A Venetian Charade

A Venetian Charade

HELEN YORK

DOUBLEDAY & COMPANY, INC.

GARDEN CITY, NEW YORK, 1978

fiction

(mystery – suspense)

7.95
DD

Library of Congress Cataloging in Publication Data

York, Helen.
  A Venetian charade.

  I. Title.
PZ4.Y62Ve [PS3575.06]   813'.5'4

ISBN: 0-385-12657-3
Library of Congress Catalog Card Number 77-92234

52352

To the Memory of my Mother

A Venetian Charade

CHAPTER 1

As the train sped along the Lombardy Plain toward Venice, my anticipation mounted. After six months of separation, after a long, arduous journey on a cargo ship from Boston, then a long train trip from Genoa, I would soon see Dominic again. He'd be waiting for me at the railway station in Venice. And in three days we'd be married—not in Boston as we'd planned, but in Venice.

I opened my reticule and removed the small, postal-card-size watercolor that Dominic had enclosed with his last letter. He'd apologized for the hasty execution of the tiny picture he'd painted, but I thought it beautiful. In a few skillful strokes he had captured an enchanting scene of the Grand Canal. The loveliest part of the tiny picture was the shimmery, pastel-colored reflections in the water of the palazzi which lined the Grand Canal.

I put away the picture and peered anxiously out the train window although I knew very well it would be a while before the train entered the railway station in Venice.

Within a short time I was opening my reticule again to assure myself that the necessary personal papers were in order so there would be no difficulty in securing the marriage certificate. Dominic had written that he would seek a dispensation to forgo the reading of the banns so that we might be married immediately. "Make sure you bring the necessary identification papers," he'd instructed, "the baptismal certificate especially."

I hoped Dominic would be pleased with my appearance when he met me in the station. My clothes were serviceable and clean but they were not the blue dimity travel costume and white linen bonnet with blue ribbons that I'd intended to wear.

The clothes I wore were donated by some generous ladies in Genoa so that I might continue my journey to Venice. The skirt must have belonged to a stout, elderly woman. It was black, made of a coarse cloth, and was too large for me, so I had to pin it securely to my camisole. The bulky gray cotton blouse might have belonged to the same woman. Like the skirt, however, it was clean and neatly ironed. The mending on both the skirt and the blouse was done so meticulously it was barely noticeable. Not the most becoming clothes for a twenty-year-old bride-to-be but I was grateful for them and grateful, too, for the generosity shown me during my one-week unexpected stay in Genoa.

It was one of the nuns at the hospital who had rounded up a group of women from the nearby parish and they, under the nun's direction, had not only gathered together the clothes but had prevailed upon the parish priest, who in turn collected enough money from his parishioners for my train ticket to Venice plus a few extra lire.

How joyously that day in Genoa had begun. My journey by cargo ship from Boston had been a trying one, and I was ill for part of the time. But when, eventually, we docked in Genoa, my spirits rose, and I was filled with excitement and expectation. I was fortunate: there was no delay in securing train accommodations to take me from Genoa to Venice.

Within one hour everything was changed. The train had barely left Genoa when it slipped the tracks, causing a nightmarish accident. There were fatalities and serious injuries, but I escaped with only a gash in my arm and a blow to the head which caused me to lose my memory for three days.

On the third day I was permitted to dictate a letter to one of the nuns on nursing duty in the hospital. I explained to Dominic the reason for my delay and that the hospital insisted upon detaining me for another four days. I asked him not to come to Genoa, because the doctor assured me that I would be fit for travel in four days.

Upon my release from the hospital I once more boarded a train to resume my journey, dressed in the clothes which the kind ladies in Genoa had given me. All my luggage had been lost. Through the nightmare of the accident, however, I'd clung fiercely to my reticule, not because of the small amount of money it contained but because of the papers which I would need to secure the marriage certificate in Venice.

As I sat now in the train as it rumbled along the causeway, it came to me that if it had not been for the accident I would have already been Dominic's wife. At this very moment we might have been drifting along the Grand Canal in a gondola or walking hand in hand over one of the little humped bridges that span the many canals.

I leaned against the back of the train seat and looked at the watercolor once more, and I thought back to how I'd tried at first to dissuade Dominic from leaving Boston to go to Venice.

To me, Venice had always been only a vague fairyland kind of place. I had lived all my life in Boston; Dominic was born in Venice. At the age of nine, he became orphaned and came to live with his maternal grandmother in Boston but he had never considered America his home.

From the time I met Dominic four years ago, he frequently spoke of Venice, always fondly, sometimes longingly. Then, from the time we became engaged a year ago, he began to talk of returning to his "homeland," not merely to pursue his painting but to launch a "business venture" so that he could paint at his leisure, and not have to restrict himself to flattering portraits of rich women. He started to write to his Uncle Niccolo, who had lived in Padua but had recently settled in Venice. Uncle Niccolo, Dominic assured me, already had many connections in Venice.

When I tried to reason with him, he would only remind me that this was 1881. "Venice is once again a thriving, prosperous nation, Teresa," he exclaimed. "I intend for us to share in that prosperity."

The only obstacle, however, was money. But when at his grandmother's death, Dominic came into a small inheritance, he immediately made plans for our life in Venice.

I waited for him to return to Boston, disillusioned but wiser, but his letters gave no sign that he intended to leave. He was confident he would be successful, although I still didn't understand the exact nature of this "business venture." It was too soon to tell what direction the business would take, Dominic explained, and, besides, why should I want to bother my head about business?

Then came the letter telling me to come to Venice, so that we could be married there. I did not hesitate; I knew I would follow Dominic anywhere. I booked passage on a cargo ship from Boston, and, until the day I sailed, I read everything I could find about Venice. I already knew much from Dominic. And language was not going to present a problem: my Italian mother had taught me her language. Nor would I have to leave any family behind. Both my parents were dead and I had no brothers or sisters.

By the time my sailing date arrived, I'd become as enthusiastic about Venice as Dominic had been, and was already thinking of it as my home.

I was roused from my thoughts when I became aware that the train was slowing down. I glanced out the window and saw that we were entering the station in Venice. The instant the train came to a stop, I stepped down to the platform.

I looked about, searching for Dominic, but I couldn't find him. I wondered whether the nun at the hospital had posted my letter in time for Dominic to receive it so he would know when exactly my train would arrive.

I pressed through the crowd, looking right and left. I soon noticed a man who was quite tall and who appeared to recognize me. He began to push his way through the crowd toward me. I was already in a state of agitation because Dominic was not there to meet me; the stranger's approach increased my unease, and I quickly darted into the crowd to escape him.

As soon as I did, I realized I was being foolish, letting my disappointment at not finding Dominic lead me to fanciful imaginings. The man couldn't have recognized me—I knew no one in Venice, only Dominic.

I continued to maneuver my way in and out of the crowd, still searching for Dominic, but out of the corner of my eye I could see that the stranger appeared to be stalking me.

I turned away quickly, but even as I turned, I could see him coming toward me. The next instant he was standing directly in front of me.

"You are Miss Teresa Weston?" he inquired in English. "Dominic's fiancée?"

I looked at him, a tall, broad-shouldered young man with light brown hair.

"Yes, I'm Teresa Weston."

"I'm Charles Voulart," he said, "a friend of Dominic's."

At his words, all my unease slipped away. Some pressing business must have prevented Dominic from meeting me, and his friend Charles Voulart came in his place.

But the look on Charles Voulart's face made me ask at once, "What is wrong? Has something happened to Dominic? You look as if—" Then, as if wishing to delay any bad news which he'd come to tell me, I said, "How did you know me?"

"Dominic had shown me a portrait of you—two, in fact. They were such good likenesses, I recognized you immediately."

"Why didn't Dominic come?" I was conscious of the rising panic in my voice. "I explained in my letter why I would be delayed."

"Yes, I read the letter; I'm sorry you had to go through that ordeal of the train accident."

"What has happened to Dominic?" I asked, my voice faltering. "Why—why hasn't he come to meet me?"

"Why don't I see to your luggage first?" Charles Voulart said. "Then we can talk about it when we're settled in the gondola."

"I have no luggage. I lost everything at the time of the accident. You said we would talk about it. Talk about what? Tell me now."

Charles Voulart looked away, then, returning his gaze to me, said, "Dominic is dead."

"Dead?" The word came out in a strangled whisper. All the noise around me was suddenly smothered into silence. I heard nothing. Then, the next instant, all the sounds in the railway station rose to a keening pitch.

I shook myself out of the dizzying onslaught of shock and braced my back to stop the slight swaying of my body. I was conscious then of Charles Voulart's hand on my arm.

"That cannot be true," I said in a dull, hollow tone.

"I'm sorry; it is true," Charles Voulart answered.

"When?" I asked in a pained whisper. "How?"

"He died five days ago. He was buried the day before yesterday, the day your letter arrived from Genoa."

"Died of what?" I asked with disbelief.

"Of natural causes. I don't know the exact nature of the illness," Charles Voulart answered in what struck me as a cold, impersonal tone.

"May we be on our way?" I heard Charles Voulart say briskly. "I have an important business appointment to attend to this afternoon. I was able to postpone it in order to meet your train." He was already walking toward the waiting gondola, his arm supporting me.

"May we be on our way?" he had said. To where? To what used to be Dominic's lodgings? Where I would gather up his few possessions? Then what? My money would see me through no more than two days in Venice. I knew no one here; there was not even Uncle Niccolo to turn to. In Dominic's last letter he'd written that Uncle Niccolo had left Venice, giving no information where he'd gone.

I was half aware of being helped into a gondola. Soon we were gliding along the water and I was conscious of the swirls of fog which hovered above the water. What sounds there were on the canal were muffled by the fog as the gondola made its way between the almost invisible poles which marked the water lanes. An occasional warning cry from another gondolier pierced the eerie silence.

I was staring down into the black, churning water, visible where the fog had rolled away in places. I raised my head at the sound of a church bell tolling from some distant church. Charles Voulart, hidden partly by the rolling fog, appeared like a large gray shadow. When the swirls of fog drifted away from his face, I saw that his eyes were intent upon me. I thought I detected a speculative, almost wary look on his face, but I checked my suspicion, realizing that my bewilderment was distorting my judgment.

I lowered my eyes, gazing once more into the black water as it lapped against the gondola. A particular thought began to form in my head: what if Dominic had not, as Charles Voulart had said, died of natural causes. The intuition was so strong within me that I could not believe anything else. At intervals, the thought that Dominic could not be dead kept edging its way into my mind. But I knew I only wanted to believe that.

I must remain in Venice, I told myself, until I can discover the circumstances surrounding Dominic's death. I did not expect this stranger with the French-sounding name to offer any further assistance. I would make it my business to locate Uncle Niccolo. And I would speak with the doctor who attended Dominic. I would also speak with the Police Inspector. But I would have to find employment immediately. Knowing the Italian language would be helpful.

I looked up as the gondola made a turn in the canal. Here the fog had thinned out into gauzy streaks. I could see the domes of St. Mark's ahead. Alongside the Grand Canal were the pink, yellow, and pale blue palazzi, their reflections tinting the water in the canal. The scene was very much like the small picture Dominic had painted for me.

The numbed shock that had held me in its grip was beginning to wear off. A wave of grief and sadness was building up inside me. I had to hold my breath and press my lips together tightly.

"Where does Dominic's Uncle Niccolo live now?" I asked. I had to speak or the tears would have begun to flow.

Charles Voulart looked up sharply. "I don't know. He might have returned to Padua or he might be in Venice. I've never met him. The landlady of the lodgings where Dominic lived said Uncle Niccolo told her he was leaving Venice immediately after the funeral. It was Uncle Niccolo who took care of the burial. Apparently, the landlady knew where to contact him. Dominic is buried in Venice, on the cemetery island of San Michele."

"Not in Padua? I would have expected him to be buried there, as his parents were originally from Padua. Dominic's father had not come to Venice till he was a young man, recently married. When he died, he was buried in Padua. Dominic's mother is buried there too."

"Perhaps Uncle Niccolo knew how much Dominic loved Venice."

"Yes, I can understand that. I hope the landlady will be helpful," I said. "How long do you think she will let me stay in Dominic's lodgings? I have very little money." The look Charles Voulart gave me caused me to ask, "We are going to Dominic's lodgings, aren't we?"

"No, we aren't. The landlady's married daughter is already occupying the rooms. I'm going to have you register at a hotel not far from the Piazza San Marco." Then, probably noticing my disappointment, he added, "I will show you Dominic's lodgings when I return from my appointment and I will take you to the cemetery island. I'm sorry but I cannot spare the time now."

"How long had you known Dominic?" I asked. "Were you and he close friends?"

"We weren't close at all. I barely knew him. I'd met him a few times on business matters."

"What kind of business?" I put in hastily.

"I consulted him concerning some portrait consignments but he showed no interest. He said he was too involved in other matters at the moment, something he and his Uncle Niccolo were developing."

"Something? You don't know what exactly?"

"No, I do not."

A silence fell between us, then I asked, "Did you attend Dominic's funeral?"

"No. I'd gone to his lodgings yesterday to see him about the portraits, and it was only then that the landlady told me that Dominic had been buried the previous day. She showed me your letter and asked me to meet your train." There was a hesitation, then he said, "As I've told you, Dominic and I were not at all close."

So that explained what I thought was a cold, impersonal attitude. Meeting my train was an imposition thrust upon him by the landlady.

The gondola was now easing toward the landing stage at the Piazzetta. The lacy stone arcades of the Doges' Palace came into view. My gaze moved from the small Piazzetta at the water's edge to the vast Piazza beyond it. I still could not make myself believe that Dominic and I would not be strolling together in the Piazza San Marco, laughing together, drinking coffee at one of the tables in front of Florian's.

I felt a hand on my arm and dimly realized that I was being helped out of the gondola onto the broad stone steps. I saw the tall columns at each end of the Piazzetta, the lion of St. Mark, the patron saint of Venice, on one side; St. Theodore at the other, on a crocodile, the symbol of evil. Symbol of evil. The words lingered in my mind.

"What did you hope to discuss with Uncle Niccolo?" I heard Charles Voulart ask unexpectedly.

"I intend to look into the circumstances surrounding Dominic's death."

Charles Voulart's eyes widened. "He died of natural causes. The doctor will be able to tell you that." After we'd gone a short distance along the quay, past the Doges' Palace, he said, "You told me that you had only a small amount of money."

"Only enough to last me for two days. I will immediately seek employment."

Charles Voulart's hurried steps came to a halt. "You can learn all you need to know about Dominic's death in two days. That will also be sufficient time to attend to all other details. After that, you should not add to your ordeal by remaining alone in a strange city and trying to find employment here. You should return home."

"I don't have the money for the return passage. I *will* remain in Venice," I said almost defiantly, "and I must find employment."

He turned abruptly and continued walking. I had to hurry to keep up with him. "The hotel is only a short distance away," he said. "I must leave immediately. Until I return, you should go to the Piazza rather than sit alone in your hotel room. If I don't find you at the hotel, I will look for you there."

"While I'm waiting for you to return, I will go to see the Police Inspector."

Charles Voulart's quick steps faltered. He swung his head around to look at me. "You're causing yourself all sorts of additional anguish. There's no need to go to the Police Inspector. When I return, I will see to it that you get all the information you need. I strongly urge you not to stay on. As for your passage back to America, I'm sure that somehow that can be worked out. And this is the hotel," he said as we went toward a narrow building at the far end of the quay. As we mounted the stone steps to the front entrance I saw that the terra-cotta walls were blistered and stained. The foyer was small with an air of shabbiness about it.

The registration at the desk was hastily completed. I handed the desk clerk my payment for the first night's lodging and, as he handed me the key, Charles Voulart drew me aside. "I'll look for you at the Piazza," he said as he left.

As I watched him go out the door, I wondered whether I would ever see him again.

I climbed the stairs to my room on the top floor.

Immediately, the pent-up anguish and sadness overwhelmed me, and I gave in to my grief. I fell face down onto the bed and let the tears come. I knew that I was partially weeping for myself, but mainly for Dominic, that his life should have been snuffed out at so young an age, when he had so many dreams and ambitions, such great potential as an artist.

It seemed I would never be able to stop the wrenching sobs but, gradually, they dwindled to silent weeping after which an intense exhaustion overcame me and I mercifully fell into a deep sleep.

When I awoke, it seemed I'd slept for a very long time. I became alarmed, wondering whether Charles Voulart had returned and I hadn't heard his knock. Since my watch had been lost in the accident, I had no idea of the time. I remembered that there was a clock on the wall in the foyer and I quickly went to the washstand, poured some water into the bowl, and splashed it on my face to refresh myself. After trying to smooth out the wrinkles in my black skirt, I rushed downstairs. It was almost noon. I'd slept for three hours.

"No, signorina," the desk clerk said in reply to my question, "the gentleman has not returned."

I turned to go back to my room, then considered Charles Voulart's suggestion that I go to the Piazza San Marco. It had been some time since I'd had anything to eat: the breakfast in Genoa had been an early one. I decided to go to the

Piazza and have a cup of coffee, no more than that. I would have to stretch out my few lire the best I could. I hoped that Charles Voulart would meet me at the Piazza and we could begin attending to what he called "the details." That little fear at the back of my mind was still with me—that Charles Voulart had no intention of returning.

If he did not return, I would remain in Venice until I knew all the facts about Dominic's death.

As soon as I stepped outside I knew it had been a wise decision to leave the solitary gloom of the hotel room. The bustling activity around me made my grief a bit easier to bear.

The morning mist had lifted. I glanced up at the pure azure sky. The air was crystal clear. As I walked along the quay, I watched the gondolas as they plowed the Grand Canal. Small, agile skiffs maneuvered their way among the gondolas. Several barges, heaped with an array of fruits and vegetables, were making their slow progress along the canal. All about me I heard snatches of the rippling Venetian language, the g's sounding like z's, the c's like x's, a dialect familiar to me since childhood. Unlike Dominic, who spoke frequently of his homeland, my mother did not. She left Venice when quite young to live in Rome. Later, when she married an American, she considered America her home.

I came to a humped bridge, recognizing it as the Ponte della Paglia. I'd seen the picture in one of Dominic's beautiful illustrated books. I stopped at the bridge railing and looked across the narrow waterway, the Rio di Palazzo, to the Bridge of Sighs. I thought of the doomed man crossing the Bridge of Sighs after having had his sentence pronounced in the adjoining Doges' Palace. I, too, had had my sentence read to me that morning. A life without Dominic.

Slowly, I turned away, and entered the Piazza San Marco. The strolling couples in their splendid finery made me self-conscious of my odd-looking clothes but, when I remembered the kindness of the women who gave them to me, my self-consciousness quickly passed.

After sitting down at one of the small tables in front of Florian's, I suddenly realized that coffee might be terribly expensive, or perhaps they might not wish to serve such a meager order. Before I could escape, a waiter appeared. He smiled and nodded when I said I wanted only coffee.

After that, I settled more comfortably into my chair and looked about the Piazza, entranced with the splendor of the ornate buildings which enclosed the square. It was like nothing I'd ever seen in my life. Just as soon as I'd had my coffee, I decided, I'd wander into St. Mark's to say a prayer for Dominic. Then I remembered that if Charles Voulart was to find me I had better not seclude myself inside the church. I still hoped he would return.

I turned my attention once more to the strollers while I sipped my coffee. I noticed a young man walking about alone; everyone else seemed to have a companion. As he neared my table, he came to an abrupt stop and I saw an unmistakable flicker of recognition in his eyes. Charles Voulart had looked at me in that way when he saw me in the railway station.

The young man continued to stare at me, then he jerked his head aside and sat down at a table a short distance away. I was careful not to show an interest in him. He made an elaborate show of reading a newspaper, but each time he turned a page, his eyes flicked my way, and his expression was cunning.

Thinking back to the flash of recognition, I recalled Charles Voulart's explanation that he'd seen two portraits of me. Had this young man also seen them? But no, if he were a friend of Dominic's, he would not be watching me with such furtive glances.

A sudden thought flashed into my mind, causing me to shudder even while I sat in warm sunlight. My clothes were easily recognizable. Had Charles Voulart described me to this young man? He'd repeatedly urged me to go to the Piazza San Marco.

Feeling foolish, I brought my racing, fanciful suspicions to a halt, telling myself that the young man was glancing my way only because I was unescorted.

The moment I paid for my coffee, I left the Piazza. For a moment I had considered walking right up to the man and asking him what connection he had with Dominic, but I thought the better of my impulse and hurried toward the hotel. For some unclear reason I was afraid of him.

As I approached the hotel, I had the unsettling sensation that I was being followed. Twice I did look back, but he was nowhere in sight.

In my room, I went to the window and looked down. I saw the same young man enter the hotel.

CHAPTER 2

I stood at the window, debating whether I should remain in my room and confront the young man if he knocked on my door. I quickly decided against that, not wishing to be alone with him. If I were going to speak with him, far better to do so in the hotel foyer. I left the room and hurried down the three flights of stairs.

The only person in the foyer was a desk clerk, who was not the one who'd been there when I'd arrived.

"Has anyone been inquiring about me?" I asked him. "I'm Teresa Weston."

"No, signorina, no one has inquired."

"The young man who came into the hotel a short time ago," I said, "did he make any inquiries?"

"That I could not say, signorina. I have just this moment come to the desk."

"Where is the other desk clerk? I wish to speak with him."

"He will not be on duty again, signorina, until four o'clock. But he left word with me that"—he glanced at a notepad—"that when a Mr. Charles Voulart inquires, I am to inform you."

"The young man who stepped into the hotel a moment ago," I persisted, "if you did not speak with him, did you see him? Do you know who he is?"

"I did not see him. I came to the desk at the very moment that you entered." He regarded me curiously from across the desk. "Is there some way in which I can assist you?"

"Yes, perhaps there is." I'd concluded from the first that Charles Voulart, who did not appear to be a native of Venice but only a visitor here on business, would not be staying at this hotel. His fine clothes indicated he would stay at a more expensive place. Nevertheless, to make certain, I asked and was informed that he was not a guest at the hotel.

"Is the name familiar to you?" I asked. "Does he live in Venice?"

"I do not know the gentleman, signorina."

Since he did not object to my inquiries, I went on. "Did you know Dominic Vetrelli? He was a painter. He died a few days ago."

"I have never heard the name."

"And Niccolo Sebastiano? Do you know of him?"

"None of the people you've mentioned, signorina, are familiar to me."

"It is necessary that I remain in Venice for about two weeks," I said. "To do that I must find employment quickly. Would the hotel be in need of any extra help? I'm willing to do any kind of work. I can also speak English."

"No, the hotel is not in need of any extra help." He thought a moment then said, "You might try the shops on the Rialto Bridge."

He told me how to get there, and I proceeded in that direction. After I'd gone a short distance, I once more had that queer feeling that I was being followed. When I turned around sharply, I thought I saw someone dart into a doorway, but I assured myself I'd been mistaken. My taut nerves were making me skittish. I continued on my way, not slowing my pace till I reached the broad stone steps of the Rialto Bridge.

I looked about at the clutter of shops and entered the nearest one which sold an assortment of art objects and souvenirs.

The shopkeeper's eager expression vanished when I stated my business, telling him that I could speak Italian and English, was willing to do any necessary work in the shop, and that I was reasonably familiar with paintings and other art objects.

The shopkeeper's reply was a vigorous shake of his head. As I turned away to try my luck at the next shop, I saw the young man from the Piazza San Marco, examining some leather bookmarks. He raised his head the moment I'd turned around.

I did not hesitate but went directly to him. When I began to speak in Italian, he smiled and raised his hand. "I can speak and understand English," he said in a genial manner. "In fact I would rather you spoke English," he said. He went toward the door of the shop, indicating with a smile and a nod of his head that I follow him.

In answer to my question, he admitted readily that he had been following me. "Come," he said, urging me along. "I can explain my reason much better there." He waved his hand in a general direction and I followed him.

There was a quick, nervous energy about him. He was of slight build, in his twenties probably, short in stature and wiry. His agile maneuvers as he slid through the crowd put me in mind of the cats I'd seen streaking along the quay and darting in and out of doorways.

We entered a campo, a small square, off the Rialto Bridge. Fruit and vegetable stalls were placed about the campo. In the midst of the market place, crowded with shoppers and vendors, stood a church.

"San Giacomo di Rialto," the young man exclaimed, gesturing to the church and smiling, "I have made a novena here, signorina, and the instant I saw you in the Piazza San Marco I knew my prayers had been answered."

I looked from him to the church, whose façade was decorated with a huge gilded clock. There was something immediately familiar about the clock, and soon I remembered I'd seen it in a painting by Canaletto, a reproduction in one of Dominic's art books.

Before I could ask what the church and the novena had to do with me, the young man continued. "Signorina, I believe we can help each other. When I saw you in the Piazza, I could not believe my good fortune. But of course, my prayers were answered."

"You stared at me," I said, "as if you'd recognized me."

He waved his arms. "No, no, that is not the important thing. Yes, you do resemble a relative of mine." He peered into my face. "You do have the Italian look, signorina, even though you gave the appearance of a tourist, American or English, I thought."

"My father was American. My mother was born in Venice but she lived in Rome from the time she was a child."

"Was?" the young man said. "Your father is dead?"

"Yes, my mother, too."

"I am sorry to hear that, signorina. Yes, it is true that you resemble a relative of mine but that is incidental."

"Who are you?" I broke in. "Why have you been following me?"

He said his name was Angelo. How appropriate, I thought. The cherubic face was framed by short black curls. Looking at him now, I wondered why I'd been afraid of him.

"I will tell you why I have been following you," Angelo said, "but come. Let us talk there. It is less crowded." He led me across the campo to a stone sculpture of a crouched figure. Some steps climbed up the back of the huddled stone figure, the steps leading to a platform. Angelo, seeing my puzzlement, grinned. "It is the Gobbo di Rialto, signorina," he explained. He pointed to the platform. "It is from up there that the dignitaries of Venice announced their decrees to the republic. They stepped from there onto a granite column and made their announcements." He paused, gazing awhile at the platform, then said softly, "One day I will stand on that platform and announce to all the people in the campo that I have achieved what I'd set out to do."

"What have you set out to do?"

"To accomplish my aim in life, signorina," he answered with mischievous evasion.

He dropped his playful manner and said, "Now, let me tell

you what I have in mind, Signorina Teresa Weston. Oh yes," he said upon seeing my surprise that he should know my name, "I know your name. I learned it from the desk clerk at the hotel."

"You were not looking for me in the Piazza?" I asked. "You appeared to be looking for someone."

"No, I was not looking for anyone in particular. It is fortunate that I decided to stroll about this morning. I might have missed seeing you."

"You stared at me."

"Because, signorina, I could not believe my luck. The instant I saw you I said to myself, she is the one to bring to the Contessa."

"To bring to the Contessa?"

"The Contessa is my aunt. Lately, she has become a time-consuming responsibility to me. I have a shop in Mestre which I have had to neglect recently because of her demands."

"The Contessa, I presume, lives in Venice."

Angelo nodded. "She has returned to the family palazzo on the Grand Canal. She had been living in Florence but about four months ago, she returned. Her reason, she says, is that she wishes to die in Venice." He sighed loudly before going on. "She has no one now. I cannot turn my back on her. It is she who has educated me.

"When I saw you in the Piazza, signorina," he went on, his voice rising with excitement, "I knew instantly that you were exactly what I'd been hoping for, exactly what the Contessa needs. You appeared intelligent. You were alone and not dressed in the height of fashion. I was quite sure about you on first sight. But I asked questions about you."

"I fail to see how any of this has anything to do with me," I said, then added, "Does this have something to do with my fiancé, Dominic Vetrelli?"

"Dominic Vetrelli?" he said. If the name was familiar to him, he did not betray himself.

"Yes. He came to Venice from Boston six months ago to enter into business here."

"You are also from Boston, signorina?"

"Yes. I came here to be married, only to be told that my fiancé is dead."

"Then, that is why you looked so—so sad when I saw you in the Piazza. Oh, signorina, I am so sorry."

"You never heard the name Dominic Vetrelli?" I asked.

"No, signorina, I never did. I have been in Mestre much of the time, where my business is located. When I was not there, I was in Florence with my aunt."

"Do you know Niccolo Sebastiano?" I inquired.

"No. Who is he?" Angelo asked. There appeared to be an effort behind the blank look, causing me to consider that perhaps Uncle Niccolo was in Venice and Angelo was following me, hoping I would lead him to Uncle Niccolo.

"Niccolo Sebastiano," I said, "was my fiancé's uncle."

"He is from Venice?"

"No, from Padua. My fiancé's parents were born in Padua and did not come to Venice until shortly after they were married."

"They have, I presume, returned to Padua," Angelo said, "or you would have already been in contact with them."

"They're both dead, buried in the family plot in Padua. My fiancé had no family connections in Venice. Uncle Niccolo came to Venice shortly before Dominic arrived here. They became business partners. Shortly afterward, however, the business relationship came to an end."

"And Uncle Niccolo went back to Padua?"

"Whether he is now in Padua or in Venice, I do not know."

Angelo fell into a silence, gazing idly at the shoppers and vendors in the campo, as if giving himself time to gather his thoughts. He looked up sharply when I said, "Do you know Charles Voulart?"

"No, I do not know anyone by that name."

"You were telling me about your aunt, the Contessa," I said.

"I wish to return to Mestre," Angelo said. "If I continue to neglect my business there, I will become a pauper. But I cannot abandon my aunt." He paused and gave me a hesitant smile. "And, since you are in need of employment— Yes, yes," he interjected. "I was listening carefully when you spoke with the shopkeeper on the Rialto Bridge. I had to follow you about, inquire about you at the hotel, listen while you spoke with the shopkeeper. I was most anxious to know whether you would fill the requirements for the position."

"Position?"

"Yes, signorina, I am hoping that you will come to the palazzo and accommodate the Contessa."

"In what way?"

"At one time the Contessa had been greatly interested in the writing of her memoirs. She stopped writing the memoirs abruptly five years ago when her husband died suddenly. Since then she has abandoned not only the memoirs but life itself. She is not an invalid," he said hastily, "only terribly depressed. You, signorina, could help to draw her out of the depression. The doctor has often said that if she would resume her memoirs, she would be rid of her inconsolable grief."

"What makes you so confident that I would satisfy the Contessa?"

"I know you will," Angelo declared. "I was pleased to hear you tell the shopkeeper on the Rialto Bridge that you spoke Italian and English. That was one bit of information the desk clerk at the hotel could not supply. When I learned that your name was Weston, I felt sure you could speak English. I overheard you telling the shopkeeper that you had some knowledge of art, which will please the Contessa and be useful in the writing of the memoirs.

"The Contessa's eyesight is extremely poor, so she cannot do the work alone. She once had a young lady helping her but that young lady is no longer available. You, signorina, are the one I have been searching for."

"Why, then, didn't you speak to me directly? Why follow me about and ask questions about me?"

Angelo lowered his head. "I was gathering the courage to speak to you, signorina. And—and I hoped to learn as much about you as I could before approaching you." He brushed back the springy black curls from his forehead in a restless gesture. "It would be helpful to you to accept the position, signorina, since you need the employment."

"Yes, I need the employment," I admitted. "I wish to remain in Venice for a while in order to investigate my fiancé's death."

Angelo's eyes widened. There was a sharp intake of breath. "You question his death?"

"Yes, I do."

"But why?"

"At present, it's mostly intuition. My fiancé was a young man, healthy and strong. Before I leave Venice, I must be satisfied that it was a death due to natural causes."

"Then all the more reason to remain in Venice," Angelo said. "You will be paid well by the Contessa. You will have a place to stay at no cost to you. The Contessa will be working for no more than four or five hours a day, which will give you the opportunity to pursue your investigation."

"But you don't *know* whether the Contessa wishes to resume the memoirs," I said. "You only hope she will."

"Oh no, no, signorina," Angelo said excitedly. "After I saw you in the Piazza and made some inquiries about you at the hotel, I told the Contessa that I had found someone who would be exactly right, and she agreed that if a suitable young lady could be found, it might be wise to resume the memoirs."

Whatever was the purpose behind Angelo's strange offer of employment, I wanted to accept immediately. If it was simply a lucky coincidence, then my problems of lodgings and employment were solved. If Angelo was somehow connected with Dominic—and his death—then all the more reason to accept, regardless of the risk to me.

Still, I hesitated. There was something disturbing beneath Angelo's cordiality and helpfulness. Despite his denial of any knowledge of Dominic and Charles Voulart and Uncle Niccolo, I could not cast off the suspicion that he was connected with all three. I still believed that it had been me Angelo was looking for in the Piazza. The search for me in the Piazza, I felt, had been at Charles Voulart's instruction. It was probably Voulart who informed him that I was in desperate need of a job. This offer of employment was too much of a coincidence.

Nevertheless, I knew I had to accept. The answers I was seeking might be found in the Contessa's palazzo, or even with the Contessa herself.

Seeing the expectant look on Angelo's face, I said, "I will have to think it over. What is the Contessa's name? Where exactly does she live?"

"She is Francesca Rogatti. She lives in the Palazzo Rogatti, on the Grand Canal. She is the widow of Conte Alfonso Rogatti."

"I will have to think it over," I repeated as I began to leave the campo.

Angelo jumped away from the stone sculpture where he'd been leaning. "You will come to the palazzo, will you not, signorina?" he said excitedly. "It will benefit the Contessa greatly. It will also benefit you."

And somehow it will also benefit you, Angelo, I thought, only I don't know yet exactly how.

"When will you let me know your decision?" he asked anxiously.

"Why don't I meet you in the Piazza in front of Florian's this evening at about seven o'clock?"

"I will be there, signorina," Angelo said. He smiled as we parted, as if he knew he'd intrigued me sufficiently.

I walked quickly in the direction of the hotel, hoping I would not lose my way in the maze of narrow footpaths and bridges. Perhaps Charles Voulart had returned to the hotel.

As I walked along, I thought back to all that Angelo had related. He'd said he'd made a novena, but despite his angelic features, I could not picture Angelo on his knees.

So preoccupied had I been that I was surprised to see that I'd already arrived at the Piazza. It was hearing the bell tower strike four o'clock which brought me to a stop.

The Piazza looked different from the way it had appeared that morning. There were fewer people about, as it was still siesta time. The square appeared serene, dozing in the hot, bright sun. A few pigeons pecked at bits of corn on the ground; their faint cooing added to the drowsy atmosphere.

I entered the Piazza to have my first close look at the cathedral. I'd had only a glimpse of it earlier that day, but now, standing before it, I admired its uniqueness, the rhythm of domes and pillars and arches, the mingling of opalescent light and glitter of mosaic. I wanted to go inside but, that would have to come later. I glanced up at the four bronze horses above the main arched entrance then turned to leave.

When I entered the hotel, I saw, behind the desk, the same clerk who was there when Charles Voulart brought me to the hotel.

"No, signorina," he replied to my question, "the gentleman has not returned."

"There was a young man who inquired about me—" I began.

"I trust I did the right thing, signorina, by answering his questions," he interjected.

"Do you know him or of him?"

"No, I do not."

"Do you know of a Contessa Francesca Rogatti? She lives in the Palazzo Rogatti."

"Oh, the Palazzo Rogatti is being lived in again?" he exclaimed. "It has been uninhabited for a long time. The palazzo is one of the most splendid palaces on the Grand Canal. I have heard that it is filled with priceless art. The Rogatti name is well known. The Contessa is the widow of Conte Alfonso Rogatti. They lived in Florence for many years. I did not know the Contessa had returned to Venice."

So, there was such a person as the Contessa Francesca Rogatti and the Palazzo Rogatti did exist.

I thanked the desk clerk for the information, then inquired whether the hotel had a dining room. I'd lost my desire to eat but, as I had had no food since breakfast in Genoa, it was time I had a meal. Even in this modest hotel I was afraid the meal would deplete my meager funds, but I did not wish to wander about the unfamiliar city, searching for a cheap place to eat. Besides, I was still hopeful that Charles Voulart would return.

I was led to a small walled garden behind the hotel where tables were placed among potted oleanders and lemon trees. Before he left, I asked the desk clerk to inform Charles Voulart where I might be found.

The two waiters were busy. Seated at the table, waiting till I could be served, gave me time to recall some things in Dominic's letters to which I had not attached any particular significance at the time but now took on importance.

In his last letter, Dominic informed me that he and Uncle Niccolo had come to a definite break in their business relationship. "Uncle Niccolo has, in fact, already left Venice," Dominic had written.

The news had not surprised me. There had been earlier indications that the business relationship was not going smoothly. "Uncle Niccolo is too old; he has no imagination," Dominic had complained. "All he wants to talk about is horses. Horses! Imagine! One does not build a fortune by working around horses. I have broader vision than that."

The difficulties with Uncle Niccolo did not, however,

dampen Dominic's enthusiasm. He was confident he would find his fortune. Venice was teeming with opportunity. There was still no definite indication as to the nature of the "business venture." Only once, in a previous letter, was there a passing remark about an import-export venture.

"But the break with Uncle Niccolo," Dominic had written in his last letter, "was a very good thing. I have now made a connection with someone who knows what business is all about. I met him today and we had a long, fruitful conversation. He is of a prominent Venetian family and has much influence. He is the type of business associate that I need."

So, despite Angelo's denial that he had known Dominic, I felt strongly that it had been Angelo whom Dominic meant.

I was roused from my preoccupation when a waiter appeared. At his suggestion I was served a dish called *cannelloni*, pasta wrapped around a mixture of cheese and minced meat. With it I was served white asparagus, the waiter explaining that it was Bassano asparagus. The meal ended with two fragrant golden plums, *gocche d'oro*, drops of gold.

When I finished my superb meal, I began to worry about the cost. To my surprise, it cost only half of what I'd expected.

I went to sit on a stone bench against the garden wall, which was out of the view of the tables but had a clear view of the door that led into the garden. I sat there for some time, hoping to see Charles Voulart.

A canal wound its way behind the high wall where I sat. Fragments of conversation drifted up as gondolas passed by. The garden was a pleasing place to sit. The two lemon trees perfumed the small area with a fresh, lively scent, and the oleanders, planted in huge terra-cotta tubs, were in full flower, the blossoms a deep pink.

After a long wait, I once again came around to thinking that Charles Voulart had no intention of coming back to the hotel. Still, at intervals, I continued to hope. Perhaps, I mused, I'd misjudged him entirely and he was a friend, an ally, and had no connection with Angelo. I had intended to ask his opinion about Angelo's offer of employment.

When, later, I left the garden and went through the foyer, I saw by the clock that it was a little past six o'clock.

I continued waiting in my room and when I returned to the foyer and saw that it was but a few minutes before seven o'clock, I returned to the Piazza San Marco.

Angelo was waiting for me. Seeing him, I was struck again by his angelic appearance. Yet, there was no look of innocence in those sparkling light-brown eyes. A gleam of—was it cunning? And the smile was much too wise to be cherubic.

"Ah, signorina," he said. "I am so happy that you have decided to come."

He was eager to leave. We went directly to the Piazzetta, where Angelo said we would board a gondola which would take us to the Palazzo Rogatti.

CHAPTER 3

When the gondola slid away from the landing stage, Angelo turned to me saying, "Let me tell you a few things about the Contessa, Signorina Weston. Your meeting with her will then go more smoothly. I do not wish to give the impression that my aunt is difficult," he put in quickly. "No, no. She, in fact, has a pleasant disposition. But if I acquaint you with certain facts about her, it will be helpful to you.

"I have already told you," he went on, "that her eyesight is very poor. She is terribly nearsighted. It is nothing which proper spectacles would not improve but"—he shrugged, smiling amusedly—"out of vanity and stubbornness, she refuses to wear spectacles. Her hearing is not sharp. That, too, she will go to all lengths to deny. Now this is what I must warn you about, signorina. You, too, must pretend that she can see well and hear just as well. There will be times when she will not reply to your questions. Until I learned through her doctor about her poor hearing, I thought it was because of her imperious manner that she sometimes chose not to respond. Now, I make a point of facing her when I speak. I am sure she reads lips. When you address her, speak slowly and distinctly, signorina, but not too loud or she would be offended.

"This hearing disability of my aunt's will not be a nuisance to you," Angelo promised with a laugh. "You will soon observe that the Contessa has a tendency to act like royalty. It is she who asks the questions. It is she who directs the conversation. At first, I was annoyed. Now it amuses me. I hope that my aunt's regal manner will not annoy you, signorina."

"I do not intend to chat with the Contessa. I shall answer her questions and ask none."

"Good," Angelo exclaimed. "That is the way to go about it. Then you and the Contessa will get on very well." He added, "Occasionally, the Contessa becomes talkative. It is not surprising, since all she does is sit in that room of hers and brood. She will ramble sometimes, perhaps not even making much sense. She's been that way only since the death of her husband five years ago. But these talkative spells will not be a burden to you. They are infrequent.

"It would be better," Angelo commented with a knowing nod, "if the Contessa spoke more frequently of her grief. I am hoping, Signorina Weston," he said with an imploring look, "that in addition to helping her with the memoirs, you will be able to bring her out of her depression. The Contessa, incidentally, speaks English and Italian. Now, is there anything else you wish to know, signorina, because we have arrived at the Palazzo Rogatti?"

"I can think of nothing to ask at present," I answered, turning to look at the palazzo Angelo was pointing to.

The sun, striking the canal, sent up reflections of light across the façade of the Palazzo Rogatti. The ripples in the water caused the reflections to undulate across the front of the palazzo, making it seem even less real.

The palazzo, of a rose-colored stone, was three stories high. Two tiers of loggias, lacy, arched balconies, decorated the façade. The carving of the loggias was repeated in the stone railing which ran the full length of the roof.

As the gondola moved toward the striped mooring pole, Angelo offered me his arm and when the gondola slid alongside the stone steps he helped me out.

We passed through a black wrought-iron gate and entered a narrow, stone-flagged courtyard. At each end of the courtyard was a row of poplar trees, tall, erect, perfectly shaped.

Angelo went toward a stone staircase, the bottom broad step of which was decorated with a pair of gargoyles, the hideous faces grotesque with lolling tongues, bulging, staring eyes, and leering grins.

We ascended the stairs, which brought us to the main floor of the palazzo, and entered what was probably the grand salon. The vast marble floor was covered at intervals with lustrous Persian rugs. The walls were hung with tapestries and paintings in heavy gilt frames. From the center of the carved, painted ceiling hung an enormous chandelier of Venetian glass. Sculptured heads, some of stone, some of bronze, were placed against the wall on fluted stands. Scarlet velvet curtains were draped at the high arched windows.

I followed Angelo into a corridor. He did not speak. When I glanced his way, I saw that his face was taut, the lips pulled tight. He appeared anxious about the outcome of my meeting with the Contessa. The flicker of an encouraging smile he gave me as he rapped firmly on a closed door did not hide his nervousness.

A voice from within the room answered and I followed Angelo into a large, shadowy room, the walls covered with maroon damask. Here, too, the floor was marble with thin velvety rugs. A Venetian glass chandelier, smaller than the one in the grand salon, hung from a gilded ceiling. A dark wood canopied bed with maroon velvet hangings dominated the room. I glanced at the large, gold-framed portrait above the bed and realized that it was probably the Contessa's husband. The face in the portrait was unclear in the shadowy light in the room but, even in the half light, it looked down at me with a rakish smile.

I drew my eyes away from the portrait to the far side of the room where the Contessa, a woman about sixty years old, was sitting in an ornately carved chair. She wore a gray silk gown with layers of white lace wound about her neck. The face was thin and narrow, the prominent nose long and bony. Her hair, a glossy black, was arranged at the top of her head into an intricate coil of braids. Topaz earrings dangled from her ears.

She sat erect, head tilted back slightly, hands resting on the arms of the throne-like chair. She did not have the appearance of a brooding recluse, waiting to die. There was a keen, alert look in her thin face. The hooded eyes were fixed on me intently.

"Come," I heard Angelo say. "The Contessa is most anxious to meet you." He placed his hand lightly on my arm and drew me halfway across the room. At that instant, the Contessa jerked her head forward. She made a sharp, harsh sound in her throat, and stared at me as if in recognition. It was a repetition of the scene in St. Mark's Piazza with Angelo.

"I told you I would find her if I searched long enough," Angelo said with a ripple of laughter. "Now that I've found her, you must resume the memoirs immediately."

The Contessa slowly drew her head back, sitting erect once more. Her eyes did not leave my face. Amazement and disbelief were still plainly etched in the angular face.

Angelo pulled up a small gilt and brocade chair and gestured that I sit down.

"You call yourself Teresa?" the Contessa said. She spoke in English, her voice strong and firm but somewhat harsh.

"Yes, that is my name."

The Contessa regarded me thoughtfully for a prolonged moment, then drew her eyes to her hands, folded now in her lap. "Yes, I will resume the memoirs," she said, darting a glance at Angelo, then lowering her eyes once more. "I did not think I would ever wish to go back to them but—" There was a pause, a long, deep sigh. "But it is best to finish things. I will finish what I'd set out to do."

I heard Angelo beside me make a sudden, restless move.

"My nephew tells me," the Contessa continued, "that you came to Venice hoping to be married to the man you love but you have learned that he is dead."

"Yes, that is true. I've been told he is dead."

"And you believe he might have been—might have been—murdered?" the Contessa inquired.

"He might have been. I don't actually know."

The Contessa's thin lips puckered thoughtfully. She lowered her head again, gazing at her hands, which she was working with a slow, wringing motion. After a short silence, she began to speak, to ramble, as Angelo said she occasionally did. She didn't seem to be addressing either me or Angelo. A vague look spread over her face. She began to talk of "forgiveness," saying in a dreamy voice that to carry hatred within oneself was a corroding thing. "Retribution," she murmured, repeating the word. "One must act upon it," she said, "or one must forgive. Yes, perhaps to forgive. Let bygones be bygones."

She raised her head and gave me a faint smile. "Sometimes it is difficult to forgive, is it not?" Without expecting a reply from me, she continued, "Still, there is the question of guilt to be dealt with. Don't you agree, Lucia?"

"Her name is not Lucia. It is Teresa," Angelo said sharply.

"Forgive me," the Contessa said. "Yes, yes, I know. You call yourself Teresa. Angelo has told me that."

"Now that you have met each other," Angelo said, placing his hand on my arm, "why don't I show Teresa to her room. She has had an exhausting day. I'm sure she would appreciate a brief rest."

"Yes, Angelo, make her comfortable," the Contessa said. She turned to look at me, a smile touching her face. "I will see you in the morning, Teresa."

When I stepped into the corridor and looked at Angelo, I saw that he was quite agitated. The tension had begun to show in his voice and manner even before the Contessa had called me Lucia.

I was on the point of asking Angelo what that was all about, but Angelo spoke the moment he closed the Contessa's door.

"Yes, of course, I will tell you," he said as he led me back to the grand salon, where we sat down in a pair of gilt chairs, facing each other.

"I hope you will be understanding, Signorina Weston," he said hesitantly, "when I tell you why I did not reveal this to you before." He stopped, considering his words carefully. "The reason I stopped and stared at you in the Piazza San Marco is because you bear a striking resemblance to the Contessa's daughter."

"Lucia is her daughter?"

"Not *is*, signorina, *was*. She died when she was about your age. You can see that if I had told you that previously, you would have refused to accept the position."

"I might refuse now. No wonder she stared so at me and looked so shocked when she first saw me. What a cruel thing to do to her."

"No, no," Angelo protested. "I told the Contessa of your resemblance. She was prepared for it. She wished to see you. Let me explain about the Contessa's daughter. She had become romantically involved with an Austrian and was determined to marry him despite the Contessa's displeasure. The Contessa expected her only daughter to marry a man of Venetian birth."

"Did Lucia marry the Austrian?"

Angelo shook his head. "The Contessa would not permit it. Lucia fled from the palazzo, I was told, and boarded a train for Austria. There was a collision and Lucia was killed. To this day the Contessa has been racked with guilt, convinced she'd sent her only daughter to her death."

"So, by forgiveness," I said, "the Contessa meant she should have forgiven her daughter for wishing to marry someone not of her choice?"

Angelo nodded. "And to forgive herself." Angelo gazed at me with an imploring look in his eyes. "Do not leave the palazzo, signorina, because of your striking resemblance to Lucia. You will be a comfort to the Contessa, not a cruel reminder."

I stood before Angelo, not knowing what to do. Questions rose in my mind concerning this coincidental resemblance and the Contessa's acceptance of it. Yet, I wanted to believe. I knew why: I was convinced that Angelo had a good reason to bring me to the Palazzo Rogatti. It was not for the Contessa's "solace" and "comfort" but had, I felt strongly, something to do with Dominic.

"Now, you must admit, signorina," Angelo said, his eyes shining with pleasure, "that my novena prayers at the San Giacomo di Rialto church had much to do with my meeting you."

I looked into Angelo's smiling face. Whatever the risk to me, I knew I had to accept this offer of employment. "You understand, of course," I said, "that I plan to remain in Venice no longer than two weeks, just long enough to satisfy myself about my fiancé's death."

"Yes, of course," Angelo agreed. "Once you've brought the Contessa out of her guilt-ridden black mood and rekindled her interest in the memoirs—that, Signorina Weston, is all I ask. I will take it from there." He rose quickly from his chair, beckoning that I follow. "Come, let me show you to your room."

We crossed the grand salon and mounted stairs to the top floor of the palazzo. The room we entered was of grand proportions. Here, too, the floor was marble with Persian rugs. I stared in amazement at the paintings which decorated the gold damask walls. They all appeared to be done by Venetian masters; I recognized a Titian and a Veronese.

All the furniture in the room was of a lavish design, the huge bed, the most elaborate, with a high, richly carved headboard. A counterpane of heavy lace, probably made in Burano, covered the bed.

Angelo directed me to a doorway. It was an adjoining bath, resplendent with marble and glittery gold leaf.

"You can have hot water brought up if you wish to make use of it," Angelo said as I gaped at the enormous marble tub.

"That won't be necessary. I'll use the washstand," I said. My eyes went to the door at the far end of the bathroom. "Where does that door lead?"

Angelo did not reply immediately. He slowly moved away from the doorway of the bathroom and we re-entered the bedroom.

"What lies beyond that door, signorina, is a rather pathetic story. That was Lucia's room. She died years ago, but the Contessa still keeps the room as if she expected her to return. Every evening she goes there to pray and to place fresh flowers on the bedside table. The room is kept locked." He smiled briefly. "I will know that you have succeeded in drawing the Contessa out of her morbid grief when the doors to that room are no longer locked, when it is no longer a shrine and the nightly ritual has ended."

He paused and gave me a questioning look. "I hope the nearness of Lucia's room does not make you uncomfortable. As I told you, signorina, the Contessa only recently decided to return to Venice. Very few of the rooms have been made habitable. The Contessa has employed only two house servants and a gardener who comes occasionally. I trust Lucia's room will not disturb you."

"It will not."

"Good. Shall I go to the hotel," Angelo said, going to the door, "and get your luggage?"

"I have none," I answered, and explained briefly about the train accident in Genoa.

"And you were not injured?" Angelo exclaimed. "How fortunate."

"I was slightly injured, a cut on my arm which is almost healed. I was struck on the head by some debris, causing me a brief siege of amnesia."

"Amnesia?"

"For only a short while. I was hospitalized for a week."

"All your possessions, all your clothes were lost as a result of the accident?" Angelo inquired. "You own only the clothes you are wearing?"

"I lost nearly everything. The clothes I'm wearing are not mine," I said, explaining how I'd obtained them.

Angelo grinned. "So that is why you are wearing such unbecoming clothes. Signorina, they are for an old woman, not for a young, attractive girl. Matalda will find something more suitable. She has three daughters. I'm sure she will find something to fit you.

"Matalda is the housekeeper," he explained, going to the door. "She or her daughter, Orsola, who helps in the kitchen, will bring you the necessary things. I will leave you now. I am sure you would like to rest awhile before we have supper."

He turned about in the doorway. "It would be advisable if you did not mention Lucia to the Contessa. The less she speaks of her, the better."

"I don't intend to make conversation with the Contessa. I will stick to the business of the memoirs."

"You are sensible. With her hearing disability, conversation with her would be a nuisance, not a pleasure. I will see you at supper, Signorina Weston. Have a good rest."

When he was gone, I gazed at the room I would occupy. Earlier that day I was afraid I might be without lodgings of any sort and here I was living in this awesome splendor.

I wandered into the luxurious bathroom, and my eyes went to the door at the far side of the bathroom, the door leading to what Angelo had called a shrine. I couldn't resist trying the knob. The door, of course, was locked.

I stood there, imagining what Lucia's room might look like. Like the one I was given? Hers would have fresh flowers on the bedside table.

A sense of unease began to creep over me as I stood at the locked door. I turned away and re-entered my bedroom. How foolish of me to feel uneasy about an empty room.

Standing at a bedroom window and looking down, I was pleased to see a delightful walled garden below. There was a gate in the high back wall. I could see the shimmer of water beyond the wrought-iron gate where a canal wound its way behind the palazzo.

I went to the bed and drew aside the heavy lace counterpane. It wasn't till I lay down that I knew how the day had exhausted me. I let my mind drift aimlessly, not wanting to think of anything in particular, but soon thoughts of Dominic possessed me and I found myself weeping, this time not the wrenching sobs in the hotel. The tears slid down my face, and I wept almost soundlessly.

The tears stopped as gradually as they'd begun, but my thoughts were still with Dominic. Instead of being with Dominic, I was with strangers, lodged in this bizarre palazzo. I once more tried to convince myself I was in no danger, yet I knew that something sinister lay in wait here at the Palazzo Rogatti, silent as a snake dozing in the sun, ready to uncoil and strike at any moment.

Perhaps, I told myself, I should return to the hotel. Even though I'd paid for the day's lodging and had no luggage to collect, it might be wise to let them know where I was in case Charles Voulart eventually returned.

I immediately discarded that suggestion. I'd waited long enough for Charles Voulart. I was done with him.

I arose from the bed. Lying there only made me restless. Fanciful thoughts and unsettling, vague fears began to take hold. I got up and emptied my reticule, checking to see that all my papers were there—the birth certificate, First Communion diploma, and a letter of recommendation from the Boston art museum where I'd been employed. Everything was there, including the money the parish priest in Genoa had collected for me. The tiny watercolor of the Grand Canal which Dominic had painted and sent to me in Boston was there too.

After I'd placed the reticule in the bottom drawer of a gold-inlay chest, I went into the bathroom to freshen up.

When I stepped into the bathroom, I heard footsteps in

the adjoining room. Lucia's room. Quietly, I crept to the door and listened. I was not mistaken. Someone was in there, walking about softly. The Contessa? Gone there to pray and to bring fresh flowers? I soon heard a door open, then close. The Contessa was leaving the "shrine."

While I bathed my face I could not dismiss Lucia's room from my mind. After I'd washed my face and brushed my hair and pinned it up again, my eyes strayed to the hairbrush which I'd found on a glass shelf in the bathroom. Lucia's brush?

Upon returning to my bedroom, I'd become increasingly curious about the room next door. I stepped into the deserted hallway and tried the door to the "shrine." It was locked.

Not long after I returned to my bedroom, there was a knock on the door. A young girl, about fourteen or fifteen, wearing a servant's apron, entered. She was a pretty, shy-looking girl, olive-skinned, dark-haired, with large, luminous dark eyes. Her tendency toward plumpness did not detract from her prettiness.

She spoke in Italian, explaining that she knew no English at all and was glad I spoke Italian. She told me she was Orsola, the housekeeper's daughter, then she placed some things on the bed—nightclothes, a towel, soap, a change of underclothes, and a beautiful gown of pale green linen.

Orsola pointed to the gown, saying that she didn't know whether it would fit but that Angelo thought it would. She then pointed to the sewing basket which she'd placed on the bed, telling me that if the gown did not fit exactly I might alter it in places.

"The gown is much too good to give away," I said as I examined it. Since Orsola was a bit plump and much shorter than I, I didn't expect it to have been hers. I realized that the linen gown, with its lavish use of delicate lace, would not likely be owned by a daughter of a housekeeper. It looked costly.

"You are to wear it to dinner this evening," Orsola said.

"That is what my mother said to tell you. Dinner will be at eight o'clock, signorina," she said, flashing a shy smile as she closed the door behind her.

When Orsola left, my gaze returned to the beautiful gown lying on the bed. Lucia's gown? Angelo said her room was kept as if the Contessa expected the daughter to return. Could it have been Angelo in that room a while ago? Gone there to get the gown?

I ran my hand over the silky smoothness of the gown, then quickly drew my fingers away. I didn't want to wear it.

I went to stand before the mirrored wall in the bathroom, hoping the clothes I wore were acceptable. The sight of myself in the wrinkled, ill-fitting, dark clothes made me reconsider. And, I asked myself, if I refused to wear the clothes given me at the palazzo, what about tomorrow and the days that followed? I could not continue to wear these clothes for two more weeks. When, if ever, during my stay in Venice, would I be able to buy any clothing? The meager amount of money in my reticule would buy me two handkerchiefs, no more. What I earned assisting with the memoirs would be needed to pay for my return passage to Boston.

I finally decided I had no choice but to wear the green linen gown to dinner. Still, I hesitated because of the Contessa. If it were Lucia's gown and the Contessa should be present at dinner, what would be her reaction? Angelo's encouragement that no cruelty was being done to her did not reassure me.

I tried on the gown. The only alteration needed was in the waist, which was a trifle loose. I remedied that by taking in two small tucks.

Orsola came to direct me to the dining room. I was tempted to ask her whether the gown had belonged to one of her sisters, but I felt quite sure it had been Lucia's gown.

The Contessa was already seated at the dinner table, looking elegant in a velvet gown of deep magenta, diamonds glistening at her throat and ears. She looked up when I entered, her eyes resting on the gown. When she raised her eyes, she nodded and smiled.

"Very becoming," she said. "Much better than those drab travel clothes."

The dinner went smoothly. The Contessa spoke only of the memoirs, saying she was eager to get started on them again. I was twice reminded of her hearing disability when Angelo directed questions to her and she did not reply. It was also true, as Angelo had explained to me, that one did not make conversation with the Contessa. She directed the conversation. It was she who asked the questions.

When, eventually, the Contessa excused herself, not wishing to partake of the fresh fruit served at the end of the meal, the atmosphere in the dining room became relaxed. Matalda, the cook-housekeeper, a short, plump woman, her black hair neatly combed back into a bun and secured with two large amber combs, had conducted herself like an obedient, silent, blank-faced servant while serving dinner. Orsola, too, appeared solemn. When the Contessa left, Matalda immediately became a loving mother bustling over the family dinner table. Her plump face dimpled into wide smiles when Angelo informed her that I spoke Italian as the Venetians spoke it, that my mother had been born in Venice and had taught me the language. During dinner, only English was spoken: the Contessa never spoke to the servants.

Matalda's long respectful silence while serving dinner gave way to friendly chatter punctuated with little bursts of laughter.

Orsola, too, underwent a change. Her face became lively. She smiled frequently, mostly at Angelo, whom she seemed to admire with girlish adulation.

When I was leaving the dining room, Angelo suggested that I accompany Matalda the following morning to the Pescheria.

"It is not an ordinary fish market," he assured me. "You will find it fascinating. You will be back by the time the

Contessa decides to work on the memoirs. She is not an early riser."

Matalda said she would be pleased to have me accompany her and I said I would go.

The following morning, however, probably because I'd had a restless night with practically no sleep, I decided not to accompany Matalda. When Orsola brought an early breakfast tray to my room, along with a blue muslin dress to wear to the market, I asked her to explain to her mother that I did not feel well and I would go with her another time.

I drank the coffee, ate some of the croissant, then reclined against the pillows on the bed.

I almost dozed off when the sound of a familiar voice made me start. It must have been a trick of my imagination. I thought I'd heard Charles Voulart's voice.

I sat up in bed, listening. I had not imagined it. I again heard Charles Voulart's voice. It was coming from outdoors. I went quickly to the window. Charles Voulart and Angelo were standing together in the garden below my window.

I thought back to how eagerly Angelo had suggested that I accompany the housekeeper to the Pescheria. So I would not be at the palazzo this morning when he met secretly with Charles Voulart? And how did Charles Voulart know that I was at the Palazzo Rogatti? How else but because he conspired with Angelo to lure me to the Contessa's palazzo?

CHAPTER 4

Not wishing to be seen in my nightclothes, I stepped away from the window. I hurriedly dressed and was still pinning up my hair as I rushed out of my room to confront Angelo and Charles Voulart in the garden.

When I reached the garden, neither Charles Voulart nor Angelo was there.

I went back into the house, hoping to find them there, but the entire house seemed deserted. Matalda would not have returned yet from the Pescheria, but probably Orsola was in the kitchen.

The door did not lead directly into a kitchen. A flight of steps, in complete darkness, led to the kitchen on the ground floor. Orsola was there alone, kneading dough at an immense marble-topped table.

She had not seen Angelo this morning, she said, nor any visitors, only her mother before she left for the market, and, no, she had no idea where Angelo was.

"I do know," she said, "that my mother will return from the Pescheria before eight o'clock. She is to serve the Contessa breakfast at that time so you, signorina, at half-past eight o'clock, can begin the work on the Contessa's book."

I returned to the garden. Charles Voulart and Angelo might have left by way of the back canal and might return that way.

When I'd first entered the garden, I was so preoccupied I had noticed nothing in particular about it. Now, standing under the mimosa tree in the center of the walled garden, I became aware of the place. The feathery, fern-like leaves of the mimosa cast a dappled shade on the stone-flagged paving that encircled the tree. The pink, tassel-like flowers filled the garden with a heady fragrance.

I began to wander about. Bougainvillaea vines, lush with scarlet blooms, climbed up the two side walls. A row of slim cypresses stood against the back wall. Where the garden wasn't paved with wide, smooth stones, oleanders grew, heavy with creamy-white blossoms. Dark purple lantana carpeted the unpaved areas.

Although it was still early morning, the day was already quite warm. The clothes I wore, of a heavy, coarse cloth, added to my discomfort. I knew now that, although I'd hesitated about wearing the lighter-weight dress—probably Lucia's—which Orsola had brought along with the breakfast tray, I might be forced to wear it because of the temperature.

I returned to the shade of the mimosa tree, where a wrought-iron table and chairs were placed, and I sat down. Even in the shade, the air was sultry. The house, I decided, would be cooler. I got up to leave when I heard a gondola in the canal behind the garden wall. I raced to the iron gate but when I looked out I saw that it was not Angelo and Charles Voulart. The gondolier flashed a broad smile from under the wide-brimmed straw hat. His lone passenger, an elderly man, doffed his hat to me and the gondola moved on.

There were footsteps behind me. It was Matalda to tell me the Contessa wished to see me. It was time to begin the work on the book.

"I am sorry you could not come with me to the Pescheria," Matalda said as we went toward the house. "Are you feeling better, signorina?"

When I said I felt better, Matalda suggested that I discard the heavy clothing I wore and put on the lightweight dress which Orsola had brought me.

I said I would, then asked whether she'd seen Angelo or his visitor.

"Visitor? I saw no visitor, signorina. I did not see Angelo

either," Matalda replied as she hurried in the direction of the kitchen.

When, shortly afterward, I entered the Contessa's bedroom, wearing the blue muslin dress, she was again seated in the ornate, throne-like chair. She wore a light silk gown, the pale lilac color drawing attention to the amethyst earrings at her ears. The sleek black hair was dressed in its usual intricately coiled arrangement atop her head. As before, when I'd worn the green linen gown to dinner, she stared at the blue muslin dress, as if the memory brought her a stab of pain, but almost immediately her face softened into a sweet smile.

"The blue dress suits you," she said, her searching gaze going from the dress to the large leather notebook I carried. Angelo had given me the notebook yesterday after dinner. "You'll need it for taking notes," he'd said. It was then he told me it was Lucia's clothes I was wearing.

"And I see that you brought your notebook with you," the Contessa said. "Good. It will be useful." She nodded to a small desk which she said Angelo had pulled over to a window so I might have light while I worked. The desk was somewhat removed from where the Contessa was sitting. Considering her hearing defect, I realized I must remember to speak loud enough to be heard.

I sat down at the desk, opened the notebook, and waited for the Contessa to begin the dictation, but she lapsed into a brooding silence. My attention wandered to the room, my eyes skimming over the glassy sheen of the marble floor, the richly carved, massive chest above which hung a painting of a madonna, its soft, glowing colors suggesting it might be the work of Giovanni Bellini.

From the madonna, my eyes traveled along the walls and came to a stop at the portrait above the Contessa's bed.

The light in the room was brighter that morning. I could see the features more clearly. The face was young-looking, early thirties at the most, perhaps younger. I wondered how long ago it was done. It was a handsome face with bold, incisive features, piercing dark eyes, and crisp dark hair. The sensuous lips were indeed curved into a rakish smile.

"You, of course, know who that is, don't you?" I heard the Contessa say in such a vehement voice I swung my head around to look at her.

"I suppose it's a portrait of your husband," I answered.

"You *suppose*? Don't you know? Look again and tell me the portrait means nothing to you."

I was puzzled not only by her words but by the harsh undertone in which they were uttered. The hooded eyes were intent upon me, which further confused me. Possibly she considered her husband as having been so important that everyone should have known of him and be able to recognize his portrait.

Before I could form a sensible response, the Contessa said in a voice which trembled noticeably, "Yes, that is my husband.

"Those ugly travel clothes you wore yesterday," she went on with an abrupt shift in the conversation. "You were given those to wear when you left the hospital? That is what Angelo said."

"That is correct."

"He also said you came to Venice immediately after you'd been released from the hospital."

"Yes, I came to Venice the very day I was discharged from the hospital."

"You were in the hospital for quite some time, were you not?"

"Not at all. I was there for only a week."

The Contessa's thin lips curled into a brief smile, humorless and ironic. "Time is a strange thing," she murmured. "It plays tricks on one. What seemed like only yesterday can truly be of a time long ago. What occurred long ago may seem recent." She looked up from her hands, which she'd been wringing. "You've had amnesia, is that not so? That is what Angelo said."

"Yes, I'd had amnesia for a short while."

"For a short while?" she repeated, then, gazing out the window near her chair, added, "Time is a thief and a deceiver. Sometimes it is difficult to know what is now and what was then."

She seemed to be rambling, yet she sounded as if she believed I was not certain how long I'd been hospitalized. I decided she must be referring to her husband's death, which, although it occurred five years ago, seemed recent to her. Her daughter's death, many years ago, might also seem recent.

I was beginning to wonder when and if we would ever get to the memoirs, but suddenly she straightened up in her chair and said, "Let us get on with our work, Lucia."

She caught herself and lifted her shoulders in a light shrug. "You will have to excuse me, Teresa, if I make a slip occasionally and call you Lucia." She reached for a folder placed on a small table beside her chair and began dictation.

For the next three hours she spoke with hardly a pause, sometimes in Italian, sometimes in English. The exclusive subject of her dictation was her husband. Her voice often trembled with emotion as she spoke of him. Occasionally she stopped speaking and turned to look at his portrait above the bed. At intervals, she closed her eyes as she rambled on, relating that part of her life when they were living in Milan and her husband had received an invitation to manage the opera house in Florence. She'd hoped to return to Venice but she gladly went with him to Florence.

For three hours the Contessa poured out her love for her husband, her admiration, and her deep, consuming grief. It was more than a dictation of memoirs. It was a eulogy. I presumed she'd gone through a similar experience when she'd related, in the earlier part of the memoirs, the anguish that Lucia's death had caused her.

When at last she announced that she was through for the day, I rose to leave. Then, because I had not been able to dismiss from my mind the sight of Angelo and Charles Voulart in the palazzo garden, I asked when Angelo was expected to return.

"Return? I did not know he'd gone anywhere. But, then, I was in my room here all morning and saw no one but Matalda."

I anxiously inquired whether he might have gone all the way to Mestre to see about his shop.

The Contessa gave a short, derisive laugh. "Angelo knows how to get others to take care of the shop. Angelo is clever. If I had not noticed that about him I would not have spent much of my money to send him to the best schools and universities. Yes, Angelo is clever. Sometimes I think he is interested only in the rewards. I doubt that he goes near that shop more than once a year. He leaves it all to that stepbrother of his.

"But I must say this about him," she continued. "He is resourceful." She paused, regarding me with a pleased smile. "He managed to find you, didn't he?" She then, still smiling, dismissed me, saying she would see me tomorrow at eight-thirty in the morning.

I went toward the door, then stopped, remembering to inquire about my wages. I had to know whether the money would cover the expense of my return journey to America.

I was satisfied when the Contessa replied, stating a sum which I knew would be sufficient.

Shortly after I returned to my room, Orsola came to tell me lunch was being served. I went with her, not to the dining room, where I'd had dinner the previous evening, but to a room on the ground floor, adjoining the kitchen. Cold meat and green salad, along with bread and cheese, were arranged on a long table against the wall. A smaller table with chairs placed around stood near one of the windows which looked out on the courtyard with the Grand Canal visible through the ground-floor loggia.

I was taking my filled plate to the table where Orsola was pouring my coffee when Angelo swept into the room.

Orsola, as always, greeted him with blushing cheeks and a shy smile and, after setting down the silver coffeepot on the table, went into the kitchen.

"How did you find the Pescheria?" Angelo said, glancing over his shoulder from the serving table. "An interesting sight, is it not?"

"I didn't feel well when I got up," I said, "so I didn't go."

Angelo kept his back to me, still filling his plate at the table against the wall. His shoulders had hunched sharply when I'd answered.

"Then you slept until the Contessa was ready for work?" he said, more a statement than a question. He still kept his back to me.

"I almost dozed off after Orsola brought my breakfast but then I heard Charles Voulart's voice in the garden. I went to the window, thinking I was only imagining it, but I saw him there, talking with you."

"Oh, you saw him?" Angelo said in an offhand manner as he brought his filled plate to the table. "You will see him again, signorina. He said he will have some free time this afternoon about two o'clock. He will take you to the house on the Calle del Pesano, where your fiancé had living quarters."

"Oh, you know where my fiancé lived?" I said, surprised. "Is it far away?"

Angelo looked into my face, smiling. "No place in Venice is far from any other place." After pouring himself some wine, he added, "As for my knowing where your fiancé lived, why wouldn't I know, signorina, since you told me?"

I knew I had not but I did not differ with him.

We ate without speaking for a short time. I waited for Angelo to explain how Charles Voulart knew I was at the Palazzo Rogatti. When the information was not forthcoming, I took the initiative.

"Charles Voulart said he got the information at the hotel where you'd stayed for a short time," Angelo explained.

"You'd asked the desk clerk there about the Palazzo Rogatti."

"Yes, that's true," I said when the recollection dawned on me.

"That bump on the head at the time of the train accident," Angelo said with a teasing grin, "is making you forgetful. Perhaps you still have lapses of memory."

"No, it's not because of the bump on the head," I protested. "I'd simply forgotten."

For the remainder of the lunch, Angelo was his usual engaging self. He inquired in a conversational manner how my first session with the Contessa went, but I sensed his nervousness.

I replied that, on the whole, things had gone well, then I told him of the Contessa's puzzling remarks about her husband. "She spoke as if I should remember him," I said, "as if I'd known him."

"That is to be expected," Angelo said with amusement. "She believes his face should be familiar to everyone, even in America."

"She also seemed confused about my hospital confinement," I went on. "She'd presumed from your conversation with her that I'd been hospitalized for a long time and had a long spell of amnesia."

"I've warned you of that, Signorina Weston. That is how it is with her. She becomes confused occasionally, particularly about time. Sometimes she talks as if Lucia left her only yesterday, and it has been years. Be patient. Do not listen much when she rambles on. Sometimes she takes medication which causes mental confusion, particularly about time.

"I see you are wearing another of Lucia's dresses," Angelo said. "What was the Contessa's reaction? A bit startled at first, wasn't she, and then pleased?"

"Yes, that was her response."

"You are sensible to wear Lucia's clothes. You cannot continue to wear those clothes you traveled in. Nor should you buy clothes. The money you will earn will be needed for your passage to America. I will give you a few more of Lucia's clothes, enough to last you for your stay at the palazzo." He rose abruptly, drained the last of his wine, and went to the door. "I will see you later in the day, signorina," he said. "I've things to do."

When I finished my lunch I went into the garden, informing Orsola beforehand that I was expecting someone and would she direct him there.

Shortly before two o'clock Charles Voulart arrived. As he came toward me, he appeared even taller than I remembered him. I saw now that, although he was of a husky, muscular build, his face was lean with sharp angles. When he came to where I sat in the wrought-iron chair beneath the mimosa tree, his light gray eyes held the same veiled, almost wary expression that I now recalled from our first meeting.

"I'm sorry if I gave you any cause for worry yesterday," he said. "My business appointment took much longer than I'd expected. I did not return to Venice until this morning. Fortunately, you happened to inquire about the Palazzo Rogatti while you were still at the hotel. Otherwise, I might have not located you."

He sat down in the garden chair on the other side of the wrought-iron table, giving me a perplexed look. "How did you happen to come to this place? When I spoke with Angelo earlier this morning, I found his explanation somewhat puzzling. He said he happened to see you in the Piazza San Marco and became interested because of your resemblance to the Contessa's deceased daughter. And he offered you the position of secretary to the Contessa? To help with her memoirs?"

"Yes."

"Angelo told me that your resemblance to the Contessa's daughter would bring her comfort. I was surprised to hear him say that. I would have thought it would cause her additional grief."

"She has moments of sad remembrance but that soon fades and she seems pleased—comforted."

"It all sounds rather incredible," Charles Voulart said.

"Angelo claims it is the answer to his novena."

Charles Voulart thought a moment, then, turning to gaze at the garden, said, "Things worked out after all." He rose abruptly from the chair. "Shall we go now to get your fiancé's belongings?"

We went to a public landing stage and in a short time the gondola arrived at our destination, the Calle del Pesano. There had been little conversation between us on the way. More than once I wanted to break the silence, to gain his confidence, yet each time I was tempted to confide in Charles Voulart, an insistent inner voice warned me that he and Angelo might be co-conspirators, that together they might have planned this charade which was to be played out in the Contessa's palazzo. All of which must somehow be connected with Dominic. And his death? Did Angelo and Charles Voulart—and probably the Contessa, too—hope to extract information from me concerning Dominic? Concerning Uncle Niccolo, too? He was the shadowy figure who still remained hidden.

"You've met the landlady," I said later as we walked along a narrow quay toward the lodging house. "What is she like? I'm hoping she'll be helpful and will tell me something about Dominic, particularly about his illness and death."

"She won't be helpful," Charles Voulart answered. If he had meant to enlarge on his reply, I had no way of knowing. The sudden appearance of a woman in a doorway nearby caused him to quicken his steps, and the next moment he was explaining to the woman in Italian who I was.

The woman, so obese that she filled the narrow doorway, folded her massive arms across her chest and regarded me with a calculating stare. The eyes, tiny and dark, kept blinking as she continued to scrutinize me. Turning, she began to speak to Charles Voulart, who stopped her.

"Signorina Weston speaks and understands Italian," he informed the landlady. "You can speak directly to her." His words sounded like a warning to the woman. I disliked my suspicion but I couldn't help myself.

The woman turned to face me once more. "So, you speak my language," she said. "Your fiancé," she went on, "caused me much trouble. I could not rent the rooms. People were afraid to take them because of his death. My daughter has taken the rooms. That did not please me. I know my son-in-law will not pay what the rooms should bring, if he will pay me at all."

"No need to go into that," Charles Voulart said impatiently. "We have come to pick up his belongings. Would you show us the way?"

The woman gave him a sour look and began to climb the stairs. We followed her into a room, the walls a dark gray, streaked where the rain had leaked in. The furnishings were old and shabby.

We were led into an adjoining room. "All the furniture is mine," the woman said. "Only those things are his." She pointed to a small pile of objects in a corner of the room.

I went forward slowly. The sudden sight of Dominic's possessions caused my legs to become unsteady. I touched the stack of books which he'd brought with him from Boston, from which I'd learned so much about Venice and its art treasures. I was conscious of a swelling grief within me but I was not going to weep, not in front of this stone-hearted woman.

My eyes went from the books to Dominic's paint box and his easel on which was placed an almost completed portrait of a young woman. There was a small wooden box stuffed with various objects. I rummaged through the few items.

"Is this all?" I asked, turning around.

The woman's tiny dark eyes flashed brightly. "Are you calling me a thief?"

"Signorina Weston is simply concerned about her fiancé's belongings," Charles Voulart quickly intercepted.

The woman turned her irate face from me to Charles Voulart and was about to speak when a loud clatter of footsteps on the stairway diverted her attention.

"Who is calling who a thief?" a young woman inquired angrily from the doorway. I knew she was the landlady's daughter; they looked so much alike.

The landlady repeated her complaint.

"I am not accusing anyone of stealing," I retorted. "In looking over my fiancé's belongings, I don't see a portrait of myself which he'd brought with him to Venice."

"It was buried with him," the landlady's daughter answered. "Your fiancé's Uncle Niccolo, who took care of the burial, said that was what your fiancé would have wished."

"What about his pocket watch?" I asked. "And his ring? He owned an onyx ring. The stone was carved into the shape of a lion's head."

The landlady, who had retreated to the back of the room when the daughter had entered, stepped forward. "You say you are not accusing us of stealing," she said, "yet you continue to do so. I do not know much about the pocket watch or the ring. He might have been buried wearing the ring. As for the watch, I recollect that he did say the watch needed repair. It is probably at some jeweler's."

As she spoke, her hostility increased, which puzzled me more than it angered me.

"I want you to take away all his things at once," the landlady began, and was interrupted when the son-in-law, who had been leaning in the doorway, came into the room.

"That is enough of this bitter arguing," he said. He nodded to Charles Voulart. "Come, I will help you load the things into the gondola.

"Do not mind the women's tongues," he said to me as he followed Charles Voulart out of the room, each man carrying an armload.

Despite the unfriendliness of both the landlady and her daughter, and not expecting much information, I nevertheless, after a long, uncomfortable silence in the room, said, "You've been acquainted with my fiancé's Uncle Niccolo. Where might I get in touch with him?"

The two women exchanged glances and shrugged in unison.

"Who was the doctor that attended my fiancé?" I persisted.

At that moment Charles Voulart, who had returned to pick up the remainder of Dominic's belongings, said to me, "I know the doctor. I will take you to him." He then motioned that I follow him out.

I decided on one last try. "Who is the young woman whose portrait my fiancé was painting?" I asked the landlady.

"That was his business, painting people's faces," she answered with a shrug. "I did not ask questions."

Charles Voulart was at the foot of the stairs, talking with the son-in-law, who apologized for the women's behavior. "They mean no harm," he said. "It is just their way."

"I'm sorry they put you through that," Charles Voulart said as we went along the quay to where the gondola was moored. "When, occasionally, I came to see Dominic, neither woman was ever pleasant but their behavior now was inexcusable."

"Why were they so much on the defensive? As if they had something to hide?" I asked when we had reached the gondola.

Charles Voulart was placing things into the gondola. He gave me a quick upward look. "Hide? There's nothing to hide. When you've located Uncle Niccolo, you can question him about your portrait and the pocket watch and the ring."

"By the way, who is the young woman whose portrait Dominic was painting?" I asked as the gondola moved away from its mooring.

"I don't know who she is. Uncle Niccolo might know."

"I don't have much hope of locating Uncle Niccolo. I

don't know where to begin. I suppose I'll start with Padua, but I have the feeling he's still in Venice."

"Sooner or later you'll come across some lead which will bring Uncle Niccolo out of hiding."

"You said you know the doctor who attended Dominic. Are we going there today?"

"No, I have some business to attend to. After I've helped you with these things, I must leave. I will return tomorrow at one o'clock. We will go to San Michele so you may see Dominic's grave, and after that we will speak with the doctor."

That said, in the brisk, impersonal tone he most often used, he removed a small notebook from his pocket, consulted it, then made some notations. After replacing it in his pocket, he slipped into one of his long silences.

I picked up one of Dominic's books and began to leaf through it, my eyes occasionally straying from the book to the enigma of a man facing me. At times I was convinced he was a friend, remote and impersonal, but kind and compassionate nevertheless. He said he had not been a close friend of Dominic's, yet he was taking time from a busy business schedule to see to my needs. Then, insidiously, the cloud of distrust and suspicion caused me to read ulterior motives into all his kindnesses, as if every move of his was carefully orchestrated.

I mustn't think so ill of him, I told myself. There'd been nothing specific to give me reason to suspect him of collaborating with Angelo—and perhaps the Contessa—but if I dared to question him openly, he would only answer cleverly as Angelo seemed to do. Or if he were innocent of any wrongdoing, I would lose the only friend I had in Venice.

I had better tread carefully, I decided. I remained silent, as he was, looking idly at the passing gondolas and barges, gazing up at the pastel-colored baroque palazzi along the Grand Canal.

After a lengthy pause, and forgetting my resolve of only a

moment ago, I asked on impulse, "Do you think I should remain at the Contessa's palazzo?"

The preoccupied look fled from Charles Voulart's face. He became alert. "Why not?"

"You said yourself that Angelo's reason for my staying at the palazzo seemed incredible."

"Incredible things do occur in life," Charles Voulart answered.

The gondolier was maneuvering toward the striped mooring pole beside the Palazzo Rogatti. Charles Voulart rose to help me out. He then reached into the gondola and handed me a few small items to carry. After loading his arms, we went through the wrought-iron gate into the courtyard.

"So you see no harm in my remaining at the palazzo?" I said as we went toward the broad stone steps that led into the building.

"Has anything been said or has anything happened to cause you alarm?"

"Not alarm, perhaps, but I'm puzzled by it all."

"Then don't worry about anything," he said as we ascended the stone stairs. "It's working out well."

His ambiguous remark lingered with me as we crossed the grand salon. *What* was working out well? Surely, Charles Voulart, so smoothly in control of himself, had not made a slip of the tongue.

"You can keep all of his things here," he said when we entered my room. "Later, Angelo might find a place where you can store the larger things. You wait here. I'll bring up the rest."

After he had brought up the last of Dominic's belongings, he appeared, as always, in a hurry to leave.

"Did you tell Angelo where Dominic had lodgings?" I asked as he went to the door.

"No, I had no reason to tell him."

He waited as if expecting me to go on, but I said nothing

more. When I asked a question, I always seemed to tell him more than he told me.

"Then I will see you tomorrow at one o'clock," he said. He was about to leave, then turned around in the doorway. "You have not been in touch with the police, have you?"

"No, not yet."

"When you've talked with the doctor tomorrow, you will see that there is no need to."

After he left, I began to look through Dominic's few possessions.

There was a knock at the door and Angelo entered.

"So, you got his things, did you?" he said, his eyes roaming over the objects that Charles Voulart had placed in a corner of the room. "That's right, you did say your fiancé was a painter," he murmured, his gaze resting on the near-finished portrait. "Painted portraits, did he?"

"Do you know who she is?" I asked.

"No, I do not," he answered, his attention going to the small wooden box containing an assortment of objects.

"I did not get everything," I said. "My fiancé's pocket watch and ring are missing, also a portrait of me."

"What was the landlady's explanation?"

"That my portrait was buried with him, that the watch might be at the jeweler's for repair, and that my fiancé might have been buried wearing the ring."

"Then only the pocket watch needs to be found," Angelo said. "Is Charles Voulart returning later today?" he inquired as he turned to leave.

"Not today. He's coming tomorrow afternoon to take me to the doctor who attended Dominic, and we will go to the cemetery to visit his grave."

"Oh, you'll be going to Padua tomorrow. Well, that's not far away."

"No, not to Padua. To San Michele. My fiancé is buried here in Venice."

Angelo stared at me, stunned. "Buried here in Venice?" he said, his voice a shade unsteady.

"I never said he was buried in Padua." I looked at the shocked surprise still etched on Angelo's face, and wondered why he should be so affected by the news.

"No, no, of course you didn't say he was buried in Padua," Angelo said with a feeble laugh. "But when you told me that his parents were buried in the family plot in Padua, I expected him to be buried beside them."

"Uncle Niccolo had him buried here. He probably knew how much my fiancé loved Venice."

"That was sensible," Angelo said. All trace of his surprise vanished. "To think that he is buried right here in Venice," he added, "and you haven't yet been to see his grave."

"Come," he said, smiling, taking me firmly by the arm. "I will take you to the cemetery now. No need to wait till tomorrow."

CHAPTER 5

Angelo tried to engage me in conversation as we went toward the public landing stage, but the agitation beneath his casual banter was noticeable. I walked beside him, reassuring myself that there was nothing to fear, yet I was experiencing the same sort of apprehension as when I'd boarded a gondola at the Piazzetta and, knowing the risk involved, accompanied Angelo to the Palazzo Rogatti.

Now I had to go with Angelo to the cemetery island. I had to know why he had become so alarmed when he learned that Dominic was buried in Venice. Why, I asked myself, would Angelo concern himself about the location of Dominic's grave? Whether it was Padua or Venice should mean nothing to him.

I could feel the pressure of Angelo's hand, firmly clasped around my arm as he guided me along the quay to where the gondolas were moored. The thin streaks of mist that had hovered over Venice when Charles Voulart and I had returned from our errand had now become a swirling fog.

Terror seized me. It was the fog, I now realized, which prompted Angelo to take me to the cemetery at this time. I had misunderstood his agitation. Would my journey to Venice come to an end on the cemetery island of San Michele, as Dominic's had?

We had reached the landing stage, and Angelo was telling the gondolier our destination.

"There's no reason to go now, not in this terrible fog," I said, causing Angelo and the gondolier to laugh.

"Signorina, this is not a fog," Angelo said. "It is only a mist which will soon drift away. If it were a real Venetian fog the gondolier would not go out on the water. Is that not so?" he said, turning to the gondolier, who smiled, nodding agreement.

I felt myself being helped into the gondola with Angelo assuring me that by the time we reached San Michele the air would be clear once more.

Gradually, my panic began to subside. As the gondola maneuvered its way through the murky waters, I could see, through the patches of white mist, that other gondolas were also plowing the canal. Apparently, the Venetians were not disturbed by a fog of this magnitude. It had been sheer senseless panic, I told myself sternly, to imagine that harm would come to me on the cemetery island.

Angelo, probably observing that I was still disturbed by the fog, which, it seemed to me, was becoming thicker, tried to distract me first with small talk, then with casual questions about Uncle Niccolo.

My reply to his numerous questions about Uncle Niccolo were always the same, that I knew no more about him and his whereabouts than when I had arrived in Venice.

I was about to ask why this sudden interest in Uncle Niccolo when Angelo, as if anticipating my question, said, "My only reason for asking, Signorina Weston, is that I feel he is the key to the whole mystifying business. The sooner you locate him, the better."

I barely heard what Angelo was saying. I was listening to the warning cries of the gondoliers as they cautiously made their way through the dense fog. Their shrill cries became a warning cry to me. I had let Angelo lull me into a false sense of security. He surely saw that the fog had worsened. Had he expected it to? I leaned forward in the gondola to demand that we turn back, but Angelo spoke first.

"There is San Michele," he said.

I looked across the murky water where cypress trees thrust themselves through swirls of whitish mist.

"You see, I told you," Angelo said, "that the fog would be lighter on San Michele. By the time we're ready to return, it will have rolled off the Grand Canal completely."

When the gondola was moored, the gondolier, despite Angelo's optimism, warned that we must not linger or the Grand Canal might become impassable.

"I will walk ahead," Angelo said. "You stay close behind. We will go to the cemetery church and ask one of the priests where the grave is located."

I stumbled along behind him, glancing occasionally at the stone monuments and marble angels shrouded in mist. I could see cats leaping from one tombstone to another, sometimes only their yellow eyes visible in the pearly fog.

"You wait here," Angelo said, rushing forward. "I see a priest near the church. I'll ask him about the grave."

Soon, Angelo returned, gesturing to a place near where I stood.

"After we've seen the grave," I said as we slowly made our way among the gravestones, "I'd like to talk to the priest. He might have been the one who said the Requiem Mass. He might be able to tell me something."

"He isn't the one who said the Mass. I asked him. And we must not linger here, signorina. The gondolier, I'm afraid, was right. The fog is not lessening as I had expected. I do not wish to be stranded here."

How much farther? I wondered. Was it just our slow progress that made it seem we were going beyond the place Angelo had gestured to? I braced myself to a stop. The fog had become thick and hugged the ground. It now occurred to me that there might be an open grave made ready for burial the following day. I wouldn't see it. I could fall into it.

"This is it, Signorina Weston," I heard Angelo call from not far away. "This is your fiancé's grave. The priest said it was between the two graves with black marble crosses." The next instant I heard Angelo coming toward me. Taking me protectively by the arm, he led me to the grave.

I stood before the still-unmarked grave and looked down at the freshly crumbled earth and the withered flowers, limp from the fog. But why did I feel nothing? It was as if this small plot of earth had nothing to do with Dominic.

I soon became conscious of Angelo's restlessness as he stood beside me.

"Have you said your prayers for him, signorina?" he asked. "Shall we leave? The fog is worsening."

I nodded and started to move away, then stopped and looked around. "I would have liked to walk about for just a little while. A pity it should be so foggy."

Angelo put his arm around my waist as we retraced our steps. "I am glad we came despite the fog. Tomorrow it might be even foggier and Charles Voulart might have refused to come. Tomorrow you will have more time to spend with the doctor now that you've been to the cemetery. If only I had known that your fiancé was buried here on San Michele, I would have brought you much sooner.

"May I make a suggestion, signorina?" he continued as we neared the place where the gondolier waited. "Do not become like the Contessa, preoccupied with death and cemeteries. It is now that you must tell yourself that before it takes a hold on you and you are constantly coming here to weep over his grave. You are very young. You must think of life, too, not always of death. You say you wish to walk about the cemetery. To look at tombstones and marble angels?"

The gondolier called to us, telling us to hurry, that he wished to be on his way.

Angelo sighed with relief as he hurried forward. "I was afraid he would delay our return trip. I have an urgent appointment within the hour."

As I stepped into the gondola I resolved that tomorrow I would return to the cemetery, alone if Charles Voulart refused to come, now that I'd seen the grave. I would speak with the priests. An odd sensation lingered with me, that the grave at which I'd said a prayer was not Dominic's.

Returning to the palazzo was less of a problem than the trip to the cemetery island. The fog had thinned out a little, which pleased Angelo. He was anxious about his business appointment and did not wish to be late.

That evening at dinner, Angelo was his usual ebullient, lighthearted self. Dinner was served in the garden. Only Angelo and I were present.

"I know you would have wished to say a few more prayers at your fiancé's grave," Angelo said as he heaped his plate with the scampi and *spaghetti alle vongole* which Matalda had brought out to the garden on large earthenware platters. "But I did not wish to be late for my meeting. As I've mentioned to you, Signorina Weston, I own a shop in Mestre. Because of my aunt, I cannot take proper care of the shop. My stepbrother does that. Not that he takes proper care of my shop," Angelo said with a humorless laugh as he poured himself some wine. "But I have no choice. I must be here in Venice.

"Every other week," Angelo explained, "my stepbrother comes to Venice to inform me about the shop. In between his visits, I go to Mestre. Today was the day my stepbrother was coming to Venice to meet with me."

"Here at the palazzo?"

Angelo's face lit up with an amused laugh. "The Contessa forbids it. Our business meetings always turn into a fight. No fists, just loud arguing. So we meet at the home of a young lady I know."

"What kind of shop do you own?"

Angelo's answer was delayed. Matalda entered the garden, carrying wedges of red-ripe watermelon. Angelo's eyes widened at the sight of the melon. He gave his full attention to the watermelon before he answered my question, saying only, between mouthfuls, that it was a shop that sold mostly trinkets, some leather goods, some silver, but mainly trinkets.

"Why isn't the Contessa having dinner with us?" I asked. "She isn't ill, I hope."

Angelo glanced up from the watermelon. "No, no, nothing like that. I stopped by to see her before dinner, and she'd already had her dinner in her room. She was sitting there, surrounded by a mass of papers. When I started to approach her, she stopped me, saying that she didn't want me to see what she was working on."

"Do you think she'll need me this evening since she's planning something special?"

"No, I'm sure she won't. She wants to keep her little secret for a while. I must go now," he said, rising from his chair. When I started to get up, he suggested that I remain in the garden.

"I will do that but I must change into the clothes I traveled in. There's a cool breeze now."

He gently lowered me back into my chair. "You wait here. I will bring you a shawl to place over your shoulders. Do not wear those ugly travel clothes, signorina," he said as he rushed off.

Angelo soon returned, carrying a shawl of a pale mossy green. I was quite certain it was Lucia's. This time I did not protest. Like the Contessa, I had come to accept the arrangement.

I remained in the garden for some time, now comfortable with the shawl about my shoulders. I watched the soft light of dusk deepen gradually to darkness. A full moon bathed the walled garden in a clear blue light. The cypress trees against the high back wall of the garden became a deep green, almost black, like silhouettes against the stone wall. The scent of the mimosa tree was more intense than it had been earlier that day, its fragrance carried by a cool breeze that drifted across the garden. My heart ached with longing for Dominic. How I wished he could be here, too, to share the moonlit garden with me.

When, later, I returned to my room, I found more of Lucia's clothes, which Angelo had promised me. I put them away, then removed from the pile of Dominic's possessions a book about Venice and its art treasures. It was one of the books he had brought with him from Boston, which I had already read but wished to read again before going to sleep. My eyes went to the easel on which stood the nearly finished portrait of a young woman. Someday soon, I hoped, I would learn her identity.

I placed the book I would read on my bedside table and went into the lavish marble and gilt bathroom to wash my face and brush my teeth before retiring.

When I had done that, I let my hair down and had begun to braid it when I stopped and stood listening. Sounds were coming from the adjoining room, light footsteps, then a low murmuring sound, like a plaintive chant. The Contessa had come to Lucia's room, to perform what Angelo had called her "nightly ritual."

I crept to the door that led into the room. There was a long silence on the other side of the door. I wondered whether the Contessa was now on her knees, praying silently. Or perhaps she was arranging the flowers on the bedside table. Angelo had said she placed fresh flowers there every day.

After the quiet interlude, light footsteps were heard again, and the chant was resumed. The pacing, along with the almost inaudible chant, made my skin prickle.

I stepped away from the door and soundlessly entered my bedroom. Odd, I thought, that she should perform the nightly ritual in memory of her daughter. I would have expected her to go through such a performance in memory of her husband. Then I recalled what Angelo had said about the Contessa's guilt concerning her daughter's death.

When I got into bed, I tried to keep my mind on the book but I could not. I put it aside and blew out the lamp. I lay in the vast, ornate bed, too wide awake for sleep. I stared at the painted ceiling, wondering whether Tiepolo had painted it. The full moon lit up the faces of the cherubs that decorated the ceiling. One of the cherubs smiling down at me looked like Angelo. My gaze went to the chandelier. The moonlight cast a shimmery glow on the glass prisms.

What am I doing in this strange place, I asked myself, wearing a dead woman's nightclothes? My eyes once more roamed the vast, splendid room. My breath caught. For one wild instant I thought I saw Lucia sitting at the desk near the open window, her shawl draped about her shoulders.

After my moment of fright, I realized that I had draped the shawl over a chair and what I thought, at a glance, was Lucia's head was nothing more than a bronze bust placed on the desk. The bronze sculpture, when I had first seen it, had made me think it was the Contessa when she was much younger.

I tried to relax, hoping sleep would come. It was the night silence of Venice that was causing me this restlessness, I decided. How unlike Boston, where, even at night, one could hear horses' hooves or the rumble of a wagon on the road. I lay in bed and listened to the eerie silence. There was not even a faint ripple of water to be heard in the canal behind the garden. No sound came through the open windows.

Eventually, despite the disturbing silence, I began to feel sleepy. Then, just as sleep was closing in on me, I thought I heard the faint chant drifting from Lucia's room, coiling itself into the deep stillness of the palazzo.

When morning came, all my restlessness was gone. Although sleep had come with difficulty, once I'd fallen asleep I did so soundly.

What peculiar fancies one can indulge in, I thought, as I went into the bathroom to wash before going to breakfast. If now the Contessa were in there, walking about, I would pay little mind.

My curiosity about the "shrine," undeniably, had grown by leaps. I must soon get into that room, I resolved. Surely, an opportunity would somehow present itself. But, for the present, I had to put aside all thoughts of the locked room and move with speed in order to be at the breakfast table at eight o'clock.

On my way to the small dining room adjoining the kitchen where Matalda served breakfast, I wore the shawl. A damp chill pervaded the house. The gleam of marble everywhere made the palazzo appear even colder than it actually was. As I crossed the grand salon, the enormous chandelier suspended from the ceiling put me in mind of brittle icicles that hung from house roofs during Boston winters.

Angelo was already at the breakfast table, almost through with his meal. For the brief time he was present, he brightened and warmed the chilly morning with his good-humored conversation. He appeared considerably elated about something, the full nature of which he would not disclose, only hinting shortly before he left that soon he would be standing on that platform atop the Gobbo di Rialto near the San Giacomo di Rialto church.

"You remember my telling you, do you not, signorina," he said, his eyes shining with delight, "that one day I would stand on the Gobbo di Rialto platform and announce to all the people in the campo that I have finally achieved what I'd set out to do?

"The time will soon come," he said, rising from the table.

Before he could escape, I said, "Aren't you going to tell me what you will announce to the people?"

Angelo darted a teasing grin over his shoulder as he turned to leave. "I will tell you, signorina, but I cannot tell you yet."

"So, you have your secrets, too, just like the Contessa," I said.

Angelo halted in the doorway to look at me. "The Contessa has a secret?"

"Don't you remember? You told me only yesterday that she was planning something in secret."

"Oh, that," Angelo exclaimed. "It will no longer be a secret to you, signorina. She will tell you about it this morning."

With that, he gave me a friendly wave and was gone.

Later, as I went toward the Contessa's room, I drew Lucia's shawl closer about me to ward off the chill that still clung to the palazzo.

I reeled back from the wave of heat when I entered the Contessa's bedroom. A porcelain stove radiated an intense heat from the glowing red coals. The windows were shut tight against the morning dampness. Three lighted oil lamps added to the cloying warmth.

The Contessa was sitting up in bed, surrounded by papers and notebooks. She greeted me cordially, her eyes lingering for only an instant on the shawl with only a reflective smile.

I went to the desk at the window and opened the large leather notebook, ready for work.

"No, we are not going to work on the memoirs this morning," the Contessa said with a playful smile. She gestured to the papers scattered over the bed. "These are memorandums of various sorts, all connected with the San Toto Ball." She gave me a swift upward glance. "Does that sound familiar to you? The San Toto Ball?"

"No, not at all."

The hooded eyes regarded me, then the Contessa tilted her head back and closed her eyes.

"San Toto is a name of endearment for Venice's patron saint, St. Theodore," she explained a bit impatiently, as if I should be familiar with such matters. "It is not St. Mark," she went on, "who is the true patron saint of Venice. St. Mark supplanted St. Theodore. It is our beloved San Toto who is our patron saint. Each year I gave a masked ball in honor of San Toto. Now, after five years, there will be another San Toto Ball."

She made a joyful sweeping gesture at the array of papers on her bed. "We are beginning preparations this morning. We must work with dispatch. The ball will be held in two weeks. All invitations must be in the mail by noon tomorrow."

"Two weeks?" I said. "That hardly seems sufficient time to prepare for a ball."

"It must be in two weeks," the Contessa said, picking up a small red leather notebook. "This is the most recent guest list," she said. "I usually invite the same people, and Angelo has kept the addresses up to date." She began to leaf through the notebook. After a long, fumbling search, she extended the notebook to me. "Here, take it," she said. "The handwriting is Angelo's. It's a terrible scrawl, impossible to read. All those years of schooling and he did not learn to write legibly."

I took the notebook and saw that the handwriting, though rather small, was easy to read. I was reminded of Angelo's remark that the Contessa was loath to admit her eyesight was faulty.

"Find the name Maria Cassiano," the Contessa said. "Read me her address."

I read off the name with a Florence address.

"Yes, that is correct. She still lives there. Hers will be the first invitation you will send. I want to be certain that she receives it in time.

"When my husband was director of the opera house in Florence," she continued after a reflective pause, "Maria Cassiano was performing small secondary operatic roles. She had a feeble little voice and an insipid personality. My husband developed her into a prima donna." A sly smile twisted the corners of the thin lips. "I want Maria Cassiano to be present at the ball. I want you to meet her."

"I am going to be present at the ball?" I asked in surprise.

"Oh, most certainly. And, by the way, do not tell Angelo that I am inviting Maria Cassiano. He will pout and argue with me if he knows she is coming. At the last San Toto Ball, shortly after she arrived, Maria Cassiano lost her necklace and accused my guests of theft. She'd never liked Angelo, so she also accused him. Personally, I believe it was that worthless stepbrother of Angelo's who stole it. It was Angelo, in fact, who later recovered the necklace.

"When Angelo returned the necklace to Maria Cassiano," the Contessa went on, "she accused him of having sold the jewels and replaced them with paste imitations of the original emeralds. Of course, they'd always been only paste, not true emeralds. She had to say that to save face.

"You must not tell Angelo that she is coming to the ball," she warned. "He won't even know it is Maria Cassiano when she arrives, since it will be a masked ball. Angelo will mail the rest of the invitations; Matalda will mail Maria Cassiano's. Matalda knows when to speak and when to remain silent.

"Now read to me the guest list. I will tell you if I wish to have any name crossed off. After that, I will instruct you as to how the invitations are to be written. When we have completed that, you will summon Matalda. I will consult with her about securing additional help. There will be no trouble there. Matalda has sufficient relatives to take care of the extra servant problem. And Angelo is familiar with all the preparations. He has supervised San Toto Balls in the past."

When, at noon, I was released from the Contessa's overheated room, I appreciated the cool comfort of the groundfloor dining room, where I went to have lunch.

Orsola served while her mother was in consultation in the Contessa's bedroom. When I was nearly finished eating, I glanced out the window and saw Charles Voulart enter the courtyard with Angelo. When Orsola ushered Charles Voulart into the dining room, I looked up at him with curiosity. There was a difference about him. He greeted me with a smile, not the wide, sunny smile that came naturally to Angelo's face, but it was more than his usual cool, impersonal glance. It was his eyes more than the smile that caught my attention. They no longer had that preoccupied expression. It was as if some problem or obstacle that had troubled him had now been removed.

I offered him a cup of coffee which he graciously accepted. Did he know, I wondered, that I had seen him with Angelo in the courtyard? I would have liked to know whether their

meeting was accidental and their conversation in the courtyard a mere exchange of pleasantries. Immediately, I put a
check on my suspicion. I had come to question and suspect
Charles Voulart's every word and move. Perhaps I should
trust him to the extent of telling him that Dominic had written to me about a "prominent Venetian family" and that it
might be the Rogatti family that he had alluded to. But I re-
considered. What good would it do to tell Charles Voulart
that?

When I told him that I had been to the cemetery yesterday
with Angelo but wished to go again, he voiced no objection. I
thought he might have then told me that he had encountered
Angelo in the courtyard and that Angelo had so informed
him, but he only said that we would go first to the cemetery
island and then to speak with the doctor who had attended
Dominic.

When, shortly afterward, we were on the way to San Michele, Charles Voulart remained his friendly talkative self,
which I found more perplexing and, oddly, more disturbing
than his previous preoccupied, taciturn manner. He spoke of
Venice, appearing to be quite familiar with it. I remembered
his telling me that he did not live in Venice.

"Where do you live?" I asked, since he was in a talkative
mood.

"At the present time in Switzerland," he replied. I hoped
he would go on, but he, instead, began to ask me questions
about Boston and America. I wanted to ask about Angelo
and the Contessa and the Palazzo Rogatti, but he gave me no
opportunity. For someone who before this had indulged in
long, moody silences, Charles Voulart now kept up a steady
stream of conversation.

Soon, San Michele came into view. A filmy translucent veil
of mist hung over the island, not the blinding murky fog of
yesterday. The tall cypresses could be seen when we were still
some distance away.

After he helped me out of the gondola, Charles Voulart

walked beside me, still making casual conversation, remarking now about the many cats that inhabit the island and that I could see slinking among the tombstones. Yesterday, only their yellow eyes had been visible through fog.

We came to a stop and I found myself before the same grave Angelo had guided me to. "I knew the location," Charles Voulart said. "I've been here before."

I stood quietly beside the grave, then, glancing up, I saw a priest come out of the church. I hurried toward him, explaining to Charles Voulart over my shoulder that I wished to speak with the priest. As I hastened toward the church, I could hear Charles Voulart following me.

"So, you are Signorina Teresa Weston, the American," the priest exclaimed. No, he answered in reply to my question, he had not said the Requiem Mass. "But I do have a message for you from your deceased fiancé's Uncle Niccolo."

"A message?"

The priest nodded. "This Uncle Niccolo came to the cemetery church the day after the funeral and spoke with me. He was put out because he had to use some of his money to pay for his nephew's funeral expenses. He claimed there was an inheritance from the nephew's grandmother who lived in America and that probably there was some money somewhere belonging to the nephew. This Uncle Niccolo said he was leaving Venice that day. He told me that he expected the American fiancée to come to the cemetery and that she might seek information. He left his address so you could get in touch with him."

"You have his address?" Charles Voulart exclaimed.

"Yes. He did not wish to leave it with the landlady. I got the impression he was afraid the landlady might direct the deceased nephew's debtors to his door.

"I have the address placed in a missal in the sacristy," he said, going toward the church. "I will get it for you."

When the priest returned with the scrap of paper, Charles Voulart reached for it before I had the chance to do so. After he read it, he gave me the slip of paper. The address was Vicenza, which I remembered passing through on the train. It was only a short distance away, on the other side of the connecting causeway.

"I am sorry, signorina," the priest said, "that you came all the way from America only to be told such sad news. Where are you staying? Are you occupying Dominic's former lodgings?"

The priest expressed surprise when I told him that I was staying at the Palazzo Rogatti.

"So, the Contessa Rogatti has come back to Venice," he exclaimed. He paused, then sighed. "She returned to Venice five years ago to give one of her annual San Toto Balls. But it turned into a tragedy. The Conte suffered a heart seizure the evening of the ball. If that had not killed him instantly, the fall down the marble staircase would have done so. He suffered a broken neck.

"Yes, it was a sad occasion for the Contessa," he said with a heavy sigh. "She returned to Florence immediately after the funeral."

"She returned to Florence *after* the funeral?" I said. "The funeral was here in Venice? Not in Florence?"

"Oh, most certainly here in Venice, signorina," the priest said. "The Conte was a Venetian. He and the Contessa had lived in Milan for years and then in Florence, but the Conte was a Venetian as is the Contessa."

"Then the Conte is buried here on San Michele," I said, "not in Florence as I'd presumed."

"Yes," the priest said. He gestured to a place on the island. "You might wish to see the splendid gravestone the Contessa has placed on his grave. Their daughter, their only child in fact, is buried beside him. The Contessa will one day rest there, husband and wife, and their only child lying between them."

I thanked the priest and went in the direction he had indicated. I wanted to see the splendid tombstone, but I was even more curious to see Lucia's grave. Although she had been dead for many years, her life had become entwined with mine.

Charles Voulart, who had shown eager interest in Uncle Niccolo's address, did not appear interested in the Rogatti burial ground. While I hastened toward it, he lagged behind. When I glanced back, he was poking around in the ground between the graves.

I saw the Conte's grave long before I reached it: the tallest monument on San Michele, the priest had said, three tall marble angels, heads bowed, hands clasped in prayer.

When I came to the burial place, I stared down at it, dumfounded, not at the Conte's grave but at the daughter's. The dates on the headstone read 1851–1855. It was a child's grave.

Angelo had said the Contessa's daughter died when she was about my age, twenty. And the Contessa had had only one daughter. The priest, only a moment ago, had said so and so had Angelo.

I read the names inscribed on the headstone, three Christian names before the family name, Rogatti. Not one of the names was Lucia.

Who, then, was Lucia? It was because of her that I'd been lured to the Palazzo Rogatti, the reason for which, I was convinced, had something to do with Dominic.

I was still gazing confusedly at the child's grave when I felt a sudden movement behind me. I swung around. It was only a cat, one of many that prowled about the cemetery. The cat stared up at me with brilliant yellow eyes, then leaped onto a nearby tombstone.

My eyes went from the cat, hunched on the tombstone, to Charles Voulart. He was coming toward me, smiling, carrying something in his hand, something made of metal.

CHAPTER 6

"I found it trampled down into the ground," Charles Voulart said as he came forward. "The beads are black, which made it easy to overlook."

Beads? It was the sun glinting off shiny metal that had alarmed me. I thought it was a pistol in his hand, that he'd removed it from where he knew it was hidden in the cemetery.

When he reached the place where I stood and held up the black-beaded rosary with the shiny metal cross, I could only stare at it in embarrassment. When would I ever stop being so skeptical and suspicious of him? I had never before judged people that way, had always taken them at face value. My shock at Dominic's death had left its mark, and my stay at the Palazzo Rogatti had intensified my unease.

Charles Voulart, thankfully, did not notice the look of embarrassment on my face, sparing me an awkward explanation. His attention was riveted on the small grave.

"A child's grave?" he exclaimed, glancing up at me. "But didn't Angelo say the Contessa's daughter died when she was about your age?"

"Yes."

"Didn't he also say it was the Contessa's *only* daughter?"

"Yes. The priest said the same. Their *only* child, he said." I nodded to the headstone. "Read the daughter's names. Not one of them is Lucia."

He read the inscription then turned to me. "Who, then, is Lucia?"

"I don't know. Angelo hadn't expected me to see the

child's grave. When I mentioned that Dominic's parents were buried in Padua, Angelo jumped to the conclusion that Dominic was buried there too.

"Do you suppose there is another daughter, named Lucia?" I asked, my eyes returning to the small grave. "An older daughter, disowned, and buried in Florence or Milan?"

"Why disowned?"

I briefly retold the story Angelo had told me. "What if Angelo was telling the truth? What if there is another daughter, disowned because she'd decided to marry her Austrian lover?"

"I believe this is the Contessa's only daughter," Charles declared. "Angelo wasn't counting on your coming to the cemetery island."

We started to walk away, then Charles Voulart stopped and turned to look once more at the child's grave. "What about the Contessa?" he asked. "Has she given you the same impression as Angelo? That you resemble her deceased daughter?"

"Now that you've mentioned it, no. I was so relieved to find employment and lodgings, I wasn't too concerned with the Contessa's daughter. When I first met the Contessa, she stared at me with the same shocked surprise as Angelo had in the Piazza San Marco. I concluded that it was all somehow connected with Dominic, that both Angelo and the Contessa had known him, and that they'd seen a picture of me and recognized me. I didn't know yet about my so-called resemblance to the Contessa's daughter. It was after my first meeting with the Contessa that Angelo told me that I bore a striking resemblance to her deceased daughter."

We resumed our slow progress among the graves. "We'll go to the church," Charles Voulart said after a lengthy silence. "We'll look for the priest we talked with. I'll return the rosary to him. Perhaps he can tell us whether there was another daughter who was disowned. He appears somewhat familiar with the Rogatti family."

As I walked beside him, it occurred to me that in the space of a short interval and without my being conscious of it, all my suspicions and doubts about Charles Voulart had faded away. I knew him to be a friend.

"Do you realize," I heard him say after our interlude of silence, "that neither of us has ever called the other by name?" There was a slight hesitation, then: "May I call you by your Christian name?"

"Yes, you certainly may."

"And you will call me Charles?"

"Yes, Charles, I will. May I ask you something which puzzled me when you arrived at the palazzo this afternoon? You looked changed—as if—as if you'd heard some good news or, even more, as if some burden or obstacle had been removed and—"

He started to laugh. "Burden or obstacle removed? Yes, that's one way of putting it. I didn't know my good fortune showed so plainly in my face and manner." He smiled, amused. "I'll tell you about it later.

"There's the priest," he said, quickening his steps. "I shall give him my hotel address. It might come in handy later."

After returning the rosary to the priest and giving him the address, Charles told him about the child's grave. "We were under the impression that the Contessa's daughter was a young lady when she died, about twenty."

"No, it was a child," the priest said. "A pity, too, since it was their only child."

"Could there possibly be an older daughter?" I asked. "Buried elsewhere? Florence perhaps?"

"Even if, possibly, there had been another daughter, born in Milan or Florence—which I doubt—you can be certain she would be buried in the Rogatti burial plot in Venice." The priest regarded us with a confounded expression. "Why did you suppose the daughter was much older?"

"The Contessa's nephew," I answered, "gave me the impression the daughter had died at a much later age."

"The Contessa's nephew?" the priest said.

"Angelo," I said.

The priest shook his head. "I do not know him. But, then, I do not know the Contessa personally either. The Rogatti family is such a prominent Venetian family that much is known about them even when one does not know them personally."

We thanked the priest and left. As we walked away from the church, I said, "When we spoke with him the first time he said the Contessa's husband died of a heart seizure at the San Toto Ball. Why, then, is the Contessa so delighted with the prospect of this year's San Toto Ball? You'd think she would not wish to be reminded."

Charles came to a halt. "The priest also said that if the Conte had not died of a heart seizure he would have died of a broken neck."

For a moment, our glances locked. "You think there was no—no heart seizure?" I said. "That—"

"—that he might have been murdered. Pushed down the stairs," Charles said.

"And—and you believe this Lucia, whoever she is, was at the ball and she might have been responsible for the Conte's death? No, no," I said firmly. "Not Lucia. If, perhaps, a long time ago, the Contessa thought Lucia might have been responsible for his death, she no longer believes that. Thinking back to things the Contessa has said to me—things which didn't mean much then—I believe that, possibly, the Contessa did at one time have ill feelings toward Lucia. But no longer. I thought at first that it was the daughter she was speaking of when she said she wished to 'let bygones be bygones.' I see now that she meant someone else. If the Contessa harbors any hostility, it is Maria Cassiano that she has in mind."

"The opera singer?"

"Yes."

"My mother's friend, Vittoria Scalzi, knows Maria Cassiano. Vittoria sings with the Florence Opera Company. She's not a prima donna like Maria Cassiano; she sings secondary roles, but knows Maria and frequently speaks of her."

"The Contessa is being secretive, even sly, about inviting Maria Cassiano to the ball. She has some personal reason for wanting her, especially, to be present at the San Toto Ball."

We reached the place where the gondola was moored. Charles gave instructions to the gondolier, the address of the doctor who had attended Dominic.

"There is something else which I haven't yet mentioned to you," I said when we were seated in the gondola. I told him of the locked room at the palazzo.

"And Angelo claims it is a shrine to Lucia?" Charles said.

"Yes. I sometimes hear footsteps in there and a low chanting. Angelo explained that the Contessa goes there every day to pray and to place fresh flowers on the bedside table."

"When the Contessa speaks of her daughter—" Charles began.

"She never has. I didn't consider it strange because I believed Angelo's story that the Contessa was guilt-ridden about her daughter's death and would, consequently, be reluctant to talk about her."

"Which brings us back to the question, Who is Lucia?" Charles said. "How does she fit into the puzzle? Also, what has happened to her? Where is she? Has the Contessa ever led you to believe that Lucia is dead?"

"No, not at all. The Contessa believes I am Lucia."

For a moment, Charles only stared at me. "That settles it," he declared. "You are not returning to the Palazzo Rogatti."

"But the Contessa has never been a threat to me," I protested. "It's as if—well, in her own words, it's as if she wished bygones to be bygones. If at one time she had reason to have ill feelings toward Lucia, she now wants to mend that."

Even as I spoke, I recalled certain disquieting contradictions. I thought back to some of the puzzling things the Contessa had said to me. I remembered the disturbing way the hooded eyes would rest on me, the odd, secret smile that occasionally flickered across her face, particularly when she forgot herself and addressed me as Lucia.

But I swiftly swept aside all that lest I agree with Charles and, in a surge of panic, leave the Palazzo Rogatti and thus abandon the hope of finding the answer to Dominic's death. I could not dismiss the intuition I had had from the moment I had entered the palazzo—that Dominic had been there. Sometimes, as I wandered about the marble vastness, I thought I could almost feel his presence.

"Tomorrow, we'll go to Vicenza and locate Uncle Niccolo," I heard Charles say. "Until then, you will stay at the hotel where I am staying. I will secure a room for you. We'll stop by the palazzo only long enough to collect your things and Dominic's. No, you are not going to remain there," he said when I began to protest. "Don't list any more arguments why you must, at your own risk, remain there. Besides, we've arrived at our destination."

After telling the gondolier to wait for us, we entered a small, secluded, tree-shaded square where the doctor's residence, a narrow house of terra-cotta, was located.

The servant who answered the door informed us that the doctor had gone to Mantua to visit his sister and would not return till next week. I was dismayed by the news, but Charles assured me that we would visit with the doctor the day he returned. "When we go to Vicenza tomorrow," he explained, "and speak with Uncle Niccolo, he may tell us as much as the doctor would have."

As the gondola made its way along the Grand Canal and the domes of St. Mark's rose into view, Charles asked whether I'd seen the interior of the church.

"No, and I only had one quick look at the exterior," I answered.

"I have time to spare this afternoon," he said. "It doesn't matter that we postpone our return to the palazzo. We'll have some coffee at Florian's, then have a look at St. Mark's. Would you like to do that?"

"Yes, but not if it interferes with your plans."

"I have a business appointment but not till later."

"Is your business directly connected with art? You said earlier that you'd come to know Dominic through portrait consignments."

"No, not art. I'm a banker, like my father. He concentrates on the home bank in Switzerland. I'm Swiss. My father is French-Swiss. My mother comes from the part of Switzerland where Italian is spoken. Since I can speak English, Italian, and French, I transact bank business outside of Switzerland. One of my clients had expressed an interest in having her portrait done. When I was in Venice, I happened to see some of Dominic's work. I sought him out and he did the portrait to our client's satisfaction. When other clients became interested, I again tried to persuade Dominic to take on the consignments but he refused. He'd become deeply involved in business with his Uncle Niccolo."

"Dominic had never disclosed to me the nature of the business enterprise. Had he ever told you?"

"No."

I then told Charles about the "prominent Venetian family" to which Dominic had alluded in his last letter. "Do you know the identity of the family?" I asked.

"He'd never spoken to me of any such connection."

"But you don't believe he meant the Rogatti family, do you? You don't think he meant the Contessa and Angelo?"

"Possibly," he replied after some hesitation, "but, even so, you must not remain at the palazzo. I know you want to satisfy yourself about Dominic's death, but you are not going to do it at such a risk to yourself."

"There is also the possibility that Dominic has nothing to do with my being lured to the palazzo. The accidental and fortuitous fact that I resemble someone called Lucia might actually be the reason behind it all."

"That, I believe, is the reason. Which is why you are leaving the Palazzo Rogatti," Charles affirmed.

We had reached the Piazzetta, and as he assisted me out of the gondola, I recalled the first time Charles Voulart had done so, shortly after we had met at the railway station, when he was escorting me to the hotel. How changed was my attitude toward him, I reflected. How his impersonal efficiency and wary manner had then given me cause to distrust him.

For a disconcerting moment there was that fleeting, nagging question: Had I accepted him too readily? Was he being even more clever than he had been previously?

I instantly put the unreasonable suspicions out of my mind. Charles Voulart was my friend and ally, I reassured myself.

"Shall we have coffee or some *gelato* at Florian's before we wander about the church?" Charles inquired. "Would you like that?"

"Yes."

As we took our places at a table, I couldn't help but remember that it was while sitting in front of Florian's, only a few days ago, that I had had my first encounter with Angelo. Then, I had suspected Charles of having instigated that encounter. How fortunate to have realized, at last, that Charles meant me no harm but rather wished to help me.

We decided on coffee and croissants rather than the *gelato*. It was enjoyable sitting in the Piazza, gazing idly at the strollers, at the fluttering pigeons. There was, as always, the overshadowing unhappiness of Dominic's absence, but I was slowly, painfully learning to accept that.

After we had lingered at Florian's awhile, we went to St. Mark's for my first look inside the church. We entered through the great central doorway. I came to an involuntary stop inside, overwhelmed by the mysterious, sultry opulence of the vast, shadowy colonnaded basilica. The extravagant sheen of mosaic and gold was spellbinding. As we slowly made our way along the nave toward the high altar, the scent of incense intensified the mysterious quality of the church. My eyes traveled along the arches to the richly decorated domed ceiling. Everywhere I looked, there was a wealth of mosaic, a unique blend of glowing, Byzantine splendor yet a harmonious, dignified tribute to God.

"The newly elected Doges," I heard Charles say, "were shown to the people from that pulpit to the right of the rood screen."

I looked up at the ornate pulpit, then went behind the rood screen to stand before the main altar, where I offered a silent prayer for Dominic.

"One visit only stirs your curiosity and imagination," Charles said when we had resumed our stroll. "It takes several visits to begin to realize what an extraordinary church it is. Would you like to come again? When we have more time?" he asked, and I said I would.

"Before we leave," Charles suggested, "I'd like you to have a view of the Piazza San Marco from the outer gallery."

I followed him up a stone stairway where I found myself standing beside the four bronze horses, above the central door of the church. From that height, the entire Piazza was visible far below.

"We'll come again to see the church, perhaps tomorrow," Charles said later as we descended the stone stairs from the gallery. "There's much to see in Venice. We'll fit our excursions between my business appointments and the details we must attend to concerning Dominic."

The two Moors atop the blue and gold Clock Tower were hammering out the hour as we crossed the Piazza San Marco.

"Five o'clock," Charles said. "It won't take us long to get your things and Dominic's and have you settled at the hotel. If we hurry, I'll still be on time for my business appointment."

We boarded a gondola at the Piazzetta to take us to the Palazzo Rogatti. I still had misgivings about leaving the palazzo, but I felt defeated about trying to convince Charles that I should remain there. By now I had convinced myself that I was mistaken in presuming that the "prominent Venetian family" Dominic had mentioned in his letter was the Rogatti family. I'd often speculated about that unfinished portrait among Dominic's possessions. It was the family of that young lady, I now decided. It was her family that Dominic had written about. But no one could—or would—identify her.

"It would be helpful if Angelo was not about," Charles said as the gondola slid toward the striped mooring pole beside the Palazzo Rogatti. "I'd like to make our leave-taking as inconspicuous as possible."

We were crossing the courtyard to enter the palazzo by way of the stone stairway when Matalda, having seen us through the ground-floor kitchen window, called to me and gestured that I wait.

"Signorina," she said, rushing out to the courtyard, "the Contessa's doctor wishes to speak with you. He is still with her. Will you wait for him in the grand salon near the Contessa's room, signorina. He is most anxious to see you."

Charles said he would accompany me, but Matalda became flustered.

"Let me find out what he has to say," I told Charles when Matalda left. "It might be important."

"I'll take care of my business in the meantime," Charles said. "After you've spoken with the doctor, get together all your things."

"There are a few I'd like you to take now." I asked him to mail the letter I had written to the priest in Genoa, thanking him and the ladies for their kindness. After deliberating, I said nothing of Dominic's death, not wishing to distress him needlessly. I removed from my reticule my few personal identification papers and Dominic's last letter to me. "It occurred to me the other day," I said, "that Angelo knew where Dominic had lived because he'd probably gone through my reticule when I'd left it in my room. And here, take the slip of paper containing Uncle Niccolo's address. I don't want Angelo to see that."

When Charles left, I went to the grand salon to wait for the doctor.

"Matalda said you wished to speak with me," I said when, at last, he emerged from the Contessa's room.

"Yes, I most certainly do," he exclaimed. "I was so pleased to learn from Matalda that you speak my language, for I do not speak yours." He was an elderly man of a jovial disposition.

"I wish, first of all, signorina, to express my thanks and appreciation for what you have done for the Contessa," he said, taking a chair next to mine. "You have been the best possible medicine for her." His animated manner became subdued. There was a slight pause before he continued. "And, considering the sad, hopeless situation, signorina—"

"Sad, hopeless situation?"

The doctor nodded. There was another brief hesitation, then: "I believe I can confide in you, signorina, and your knowing the unfortunate situation will, hopefully, cause you to become even more solicitous toward the Contessa.

"The Contessa has not long to live," he said. "The pity of it is that she had not consulted a doctor earlier . . ." He shrugged and sighed. "But she is inordinately proud and stubborn. She refused to admit to herself the existence of the problem."

Like her failing eyesight, I thought, and her impaired hearing.

"And you, signorina," the doctor continued, "have made her last days more bearable."

"Last days? She is that ill? She doesn't appear to be."

"Ah, signorina, you wouldn't believe the iron will of that woman. It is that strong will of hers more than my medication that has given her additional time. But—there is little time left, signorina, and she knows it."

"She knows it? Then that is why she is so determined to hold the San Toto Ball? Knowing it will be her last?"

"That is even more involved," the doctor replied. "Oh, lest I forget, signorina, by no means must you tell the nephew, Angelo, that the Contessa has only a short time to live. For some reason, she does not wish him to know. In fact, she does not want anyone to know. I am telling you this in confidence since you have made her so much happier than she was only days ago. There was a worry of some kind which plagued her, the nature of which she would not reveal to me. I knew her depression was not due entirely to her knowledge that her death was near. There was something more. True, she had become morbid and depressed about her husband's death. She still speaks of him frequently."

"Does she also speak of Lucia?"

"Lucia?" The doctor shook his head. "She has never mentioned that name, signorina. But, then, I know none of her acquaintances. She has been under my care only since she returned to Venice about four months ago. I know she'd lived in Milan and most recently in Florence. This Lucia might be an acquaintance from her previous residences. It must not be a close acquaintance, signorina, or she would have mentioned the person to me.

"Now, about this San Toto Ball," the doctor went on. "The Contessa knows she may possibly linger for months but that, more likely, she has less than a month, so she is determined to hold the San Toto Ball immediately. I know it will exhaust her but the ball means much to her. It will be her final joy."

"How can she be joyful," I inquired, "knowing that her husband died during the San Toto Ball?"

"I must confess, signorina, I do not understand fully because the Contessa reveals only so much to me. I did not know her five years ago when her husband died. I was, in fact, living in Rome then, and I did not return to Venice until a year ago. I do know this—she no longer fears death and she is no longer in deep mourning concerning her husband's death. It's as if she's come to terms about something and now looks forward to the day when she will join him."

"And her daughter? Does the Contessa appear happy to be joining her soon? Does she speak frequently of her?"

"No, only on rare occasion does she mention the deceased daughter. It was many years ago that the child died."

He rose to leave, telling me again how pleased and grateful he was for making the Contessa's last days so pleasant, then reminded me to keep the nature of her illness confidential.

"Now, if you would be kind enough to go to the Contessa," he said. "She wishes to speak with you, about the San Toto Ball, I think. Within a half hour, the medication I gave her will take effect and she will be fast asleep," he said as he went away.

The Contessa's voice already sounded drowsy when I rapped on her door.

"Where have you been?" she inquired when I entered. "I sent for you a long time ago. Matalda said you were not in."

"I've been to the cemetery."

"To the cemetery?" She raised her head from the pillows. "Then you saw the splendid monument I've erected to my husband." She lapsed into silence, staring awhile into space, then said, "I will one day lie next to him with our daughter resting between us."

I could not resist asking, "Was she your only child?"

The Contessa nodded. "Our only child. I never had the son I'd hoped to give my husband, and our only daughter was taken away from us when only four years old."

She dropped her head back against the pillows, as if the drugged sleep had already claimed her. I went to the door, then stopped when I heard her say, "I'd asked for you so I may tell you about your costume for the San Toto Ball. Find Angelo. He is somewhere about. Tell him to get the costume. He'll know which one. I've already spoken to him about it. And tell him to find the mask which goes with the costume.

Go," she said. "I want you to try on the costume. I wish to see how it looks on you."

When I left the room, I heard footsteps in the grand salon. I rushed ahead, expecting it to be Charles, but it was Angelo.

"Ah, there you are, signorina. I have something to tell you. I hope I have done the right thing." He gave me a hesitant grin and brushed back the springy black curls from his forehead with an awkward, self-conscious gesture. "Since you have not yet spoken with the Police Inspector, signorina, I have taken the liberty of asking him to stop by the palazzo.

"You have been remiss, Signorina Weston," he said, the light brown eyes flashing indignation. "You should have already done something definite about locating this Uncle Niccolo who, certainly, might have some vital information. I have invited the Police Inspector to the palazzo. He will be coming by shortly. I am sure he will not only be helpful in your search for Uncle Niccolo but will also provide you with information about your fiancé's death."

"I suppose I should have already spoken with the Police Inspector," I replied lamely.

"You surely have already spoken with the doctor who attended your fiancé, have you not?" Angelo inquired.

"Charles Voulart took me to the doctor's place of residence today, but the servant said the doctor was away and would not return until next week."

"*Dio mio!*" Angelo exclaimed. "Did you immediately believe that, signorina? It could be that you are being deceived. That is another good reason for the Police Inspector to come by," he declared. "He will tell the truth." He thought a moment, then said, "Perhaps you should not be seeing so much of this Charles Voulart person, signorina." He hesitated, giving me an imploring look. "I hope I have not overstepped myself by inviting the Police Inspector to the palazzo. The sooner you locate this Uncle Niccolo," he added sternly, "the sooner will you obtain vital information."

"Thank you. I will speak with the Police Inspector when

he arrives. Now there is something the Contessa wishes you to do." I told him about the costume and mask. "The Contessa said you'd know which ones." Since I would soon be leaving the palazzo, there was no reason to see about the costume, but I was hopeful that for the few remaining minutes Angelo might reveal something of consequence.

"Yes, I know which costume, a gold-colored medieval gown," Angelo said. "Come along, signorina. While I look through the trunks for the costume, you can search for the mask. There are several cartons in one of the storage rooms. I know the masks are in one of those cartons."

We crossed the grand salon, and as we entered a long, unfamiliar passageway, I wondered whether Charles was due to return. No, I decided; I'd been with the Contessa for only a few minutes and no more than ten or fifteen with the doctor. Charles couldn't have completed his business that quickly.

"This, I believe, is the storage room," Angelo said. "The Contessa had Matalda inspect the gown and mask and report on their condition."

We entered a dusty, cluttered room stuffed with trunks, boxes, and rows of cartons placed on shelves.

Angelo began to rummage through a trunk. "Look into those cartons on the shelves," he said, gesturing.

The first four cartons held quite an assortment—ribbons, old letters, keys, but no masks. The next one did contain masks but not the one Angelo said I was to wear, a gold-colored one with black-beaded trim. When I lifted the lid of the next carton, I uttered a sharp cry. The carton contained not only Dominic's pocket watch but two other possessions of his which I'd forgotten about but immediately recognized—a small alabaster patron saint figurine and a slim red leather-bound book about Carpaccio.

I heard Angelo cross the room but I did not look up. I was gazing at Dominic's familiar signature on the book's flyleaf.

"What is it, signorina?" Angelo inquired. "Why do you stare so at the book? Why did you cry out?"

"This book belonged to my fiancé. There are other possessions of his in this carton."

"How can that be?" Angelo said. He was now standing beside me. I could hear the quiver in his voice. There was a sharp intake of breath when I drew the pocket watch out of the carton and flipped it open to reveal my picture inside the watch case.

"There must be some explanation," Angelo said under his breath. "It is unmistakably your fiancé's watch. It contains your picture."

"Even without my picture, I would have recognized it, just as I recognized the little patron saint figurine and the book."

The room became very still. Angelo stood rigidly quiet, staring down at the objects I'd removed from the carton.

"There must be some explanation," he said, once more under his breath. "Has—has the Contessa ever—has she ever given you the impression that—that she'd known your fiancé? Had she ever said anything to lead you to believe that he might have been here at the palazzo?"

"She's never mentioned him."

"You wait here, signorina," Angelo said, springing toward the door, his face contorted with confusion. "I will speak with Matalda. We cannot question the Contessa now. The doctor was with her a while ago and he always gives her some sleeping medicine to quiet her nerves."

While he was gone, I searched the cluttered room and soon found, hidden behind a large trunk, the portrait of me which the landlady's daughter had said was buried with Dominic.

Soon, Angelo returned, smiling, no longer the least perturbed. Orsola was with him. It was she who appeared upset. Her dark eyes flitted from Angelo to me as she hovered near the door.

"Now, Orsola, tell Signorina Weston how those things came to be in this room," Angelo prodded.

Orsola flicked her tongue across her lips, then proceeded to explain that the landlady where the signorina's fiancé had lived had brought those things to the palazzo. The landlady had found the things after the signorina had been to the lodgings. "And I brought them here to this storage room because the signorina's room was already cluttered with many things," she mumbled, staring at the floor. "I did not think it would cause any trouble."

"So there, the mystery is solved," Angelo exclaimed, dismissing Orsola, who scampered away.

"I also found that," I said, pointing to the portrait which I'd leaned against a far wall.

Angelo swung around to look at the portrait. For some time he stood gazing at it. "It is a superb likeness, signorina. Your fiancé was a fine artist. I asked Orsola what she'd brought to this room but she must have forgotten about the portrait. She'd become upset when I questioned her, thinking she'd done something terrible. I guess she forgot about the portrait. Now, only your fiancé's ring needs to be located."

"Ring?"

Angelo smiled. "There you go again, forgetting. Sometimes that spell of amnesia which you had creeps back, doesn't it? Don't you remember telling me that your fiancé owned an onyx ring with the stone carved into a lion's head? You said the ring was not among his possessions, that the landlady said he was probably buried wearing the ring."

I tried to recall whether or not I'd ever described the ring to Angelo. I could not remember. "Yes, only the ring needs to be located," I said.

"Now let us look for that costume and the mask," Angelo said, his manner light and carefree once more.

I soon located the mask, but Angelo could not find the costume.

"I should have thought of it sooner," Angelo said after he'd gone through two trunks. "The Contessa probably told Matalda to air the costume. She described it so Matalda would know which one." He went to the door. "Come, signorina, we will place your fiancé's things in your room then consult with Matalda."

When we entered the kitchen, Orsola was alone, at the stove, stirring pasta in a large kettle. When she saw us enter, her usual ingenuous, shy demeanor once again assumed the skittish expression she bore when she had explained about the presence of Dominic's things in the storage room.

In response to Angelo's question, Orsola said she knew about the costume, that her mother brought it down from that storage room to air it, but she did not know where it was.

"Where is your mother now?" Angelo inquired.

"Down in the cellars. She went there to get some wine to have on hand when the Police Inspector calls later."

"Take the signorina to your mother," Angelo said. "I want Signorina Weston to see what a fine wine cellar the Palazzo Rogatti possesses."

Orsola beckoned me to follow her through a low, wide door. I hesitated, then went with her, overlooking the flutter of apprehension at the prospect of descending to the lower parts of the palazzo. Not that I was afraid of cellars. There were plenty of those in Boston houses. It was the apparent collusion between Orsola and Angelo that made me hesitate.

When we reached the bottom of the stone steps, I shrank back and cried out. Something soft and swift had brushed against my leg, becoming tangled for a moment in the folds of my long skirt.

"It is only a mouse, signorina," Orsola said, her eyes shining with amusement. "The Contessa refuses to have cats in the palazzo. So there are mice."

I regretted now that I had agreed to accompany Orsola. The fetid, dank air and murky darkness of the cellars made me uneasy.

"Come," Orsola commanded, taking me by the arm and pulling me along. "I cannot stay down here for long. I must return to the kitchen. Angelo would be upset if I let the pasta boil too long and it became soft.

"You are not afraid of the dark, are you, signorina?" Orsola teased as she nudged me forward. In the semidarkness, her eyes still gleamed with amusement. "There is nothing to be afraid of down here, signorina. I come down here frequently."

She was gently but firmly guiding me along a stone-walled maze through half-dark, narrow spaces. When we turned a corner, I could see a shaft of light at the end of the tunnel-like passageway.

Orsola came to a stop.

"She is there," Orsola said, pointing ahead. She then turned and began to run in the direction from where we'd come. "I must hurry back to the kitchen," she called to me. "Keep walking straight ahead, signorina. She is there."

The next instant I heard Orsola's quick scrabble up the stone steps, which seemed far away.

I started to go forward toward the shaft of light at the end of the narrow passageway. I came to a stop. All at once, the deep stillness surrounding me was broken. I heard the soft strains of a chant—the haunting dirge I'd heard in what was once Lucia's room.

CHAPTER 7

I turned abruptly, poised to run in the opposite direction, away from the chant, which echoed eerily off the stone walls.

But I remained. What was it I was afraid of? I asked myself sternly. Surely I didn't believe Orsola and Angelo had lured me down to the cellars so I would be confronted by some monstrous and dangerous being held captive there.

It was only the Contessa that I would find at the far end of the passageway. It was the Contessa, after all, whom I'd heard chanting that hymn each time she visited the "shrine" which adjoined my room, a shrine not for a young lady but for a child.

Then reason dismissed that explanation. Would the Contessa, in frail health, almost restricted to her room, come down to the cellars?

Slowly, I went forward, reassuring myself that the Contessa had, nevertheless, accompanied Matalda to the wine cellar.

It can't be the Contessa, I suddenly remembered. I left her only a short time ago, almost fully asleep from the medication.

I continued forward. I wasn't going to believe it was anyone but Matalda in the cellars, still hidden from view. The low chant began again, coiling itself softly around the stone-walled darkness.

I'd almost reached the shaft of light at the end of the passageway when Matalda appeared. She drew back, startled. "Signorina," she cried. "I was not expecting to see you. Why are you here?"

Having regained my composure, I explained that I was to

see her about the ball costume. "Angelo thought it was also an opportunity for me to see the Rogatti wine cellar," I added. "He appeared quite proud of it."

"He should be proud," Matalda affirmed. "Come, signorina." She beckoned me to follow her. "I have just come from the wine cellar," she said over her shoulder. "The Police Inspector is paying a call. Angelo said to serve him some of the better wine.

"It is a small cellar," she went on as I trailed after her through the semidarkness, "but the Contessa has seen to it that it is a choice selection."

We came to a large iron door. Matalda asked me to hold the bottle of wine which she was carrying, then, with both hands, she pulled open the heavy iron door. We entered a surprisingly dry room. Sunlight filtered in through a window placed close to the ceiling. It was a clean, orderly room. Sacks and bins of provisions, mostly pasta, were placed into white-washed niches in the walls.

I wheeled about when I heard the heavy iron door slam shut.

"To keep out the mice," Matalda explained. She crossed the storage room and swung open another heavy metal door, jerking her head that I follow.

When she closed that door behind her, we stood in darkness. Her hand circled mine. "This way, signorina," she said, directing me along a cold, shadowy corridor. Presently we came to the wine cellar, where rows of bottles in wooden racks glistened in the gloomy darkness.

Matalda proudly pointed to some bottles to which wisps of cobweb clung. "They are the finest, signorina. The Contessa had ordered that they be served at the San Toto Ball."

She paused, thinking, the plump, pleasant face turning sad. "The Contessa is such a fine lady, kind and generous," she murmured. "A pity she should be so ill. I believe she is more seriously ill than the doctor tells me. The Contessa is too kind, signorina," she added after a pause, her eyes flashing with indignation. "She permits Angelo to take advantage of her. Oh, the Contessa is not a foolish woman but Angelo is much too clever. The Contessa has done so much for him, educated him, given him money. But he is never satisfied."

I was puzzled at Matalda's displeasure with Angelo. She'd previously given the impression that she looked upon him as a future son-in-law.

"The Contessa has warned me about Angelo and my Orsola," Matalda said in a burst of fury. "But what can I do, signorina?" she said, clutching the wine bottle so tightly I expected it to shatter in her hands.

"Perhaps Orsola only admires Angelo," I began, but Matalda shook her head. "I have found them there more than once," she said, jerking her head toward the storage room beyond the wine cellar—"*I come down here frequently*," Orsola said to me a while ago.

"Ah yes," she hissed, "when I have found them, Angelo, he gives me that big, beautiful smile and says that he had come to carry the sack of pasta for Orsola. Oh, the Contessa has warned me about Angelo. She warned me that Angelo will not marry my Orsola."

"Would you want Orsola to marry Angelo?" I blurted.

Matalda gaped at me without understanding. "But he would not," she replied after a blank stare. "There is a certain young lady by the name of Fiora, who lives on the island of Murano. I have met this young lady of Angelo's. She is nothing, signorina. Nothing. Angelo is a Rogatti. Like the Contessa. Why would Angelo wish to marry this Fiora? But he will marry Fiora," Matalda wailed. "I was talking with him earlier today and when I jokingly said to him that it was time he began to consider marriage, he answered that yes, he and Fiora will soon be married. He and Fiora, signorina. My Orsola is not good enough for him? He has known this Fiora for a long time but he has never had the time or inclination to be married. But when"—her voice faltered—"but when he has made my Orsola unfit to marry anyone else, then he will marry Fiora immediately."

"Wouldn't it help matters," I said, breaking into Matalda's agonized complaint, "if Orsola was removed from the Palazzo Rogatti? Couldn't Orsola secure employment elsewhere?"

Matalda heaved a loud, deep sigh. "But where, signorina? I will not abandon the Contessa. And the Contessa is well pleased with Orsola. My Orsola is a good worker."

"Perhaps I could ask a friend of mine to find other employment for Orsola," I suggested rashly. "I'm speaking of Charles Voulart."

Matalda's plump face dimpled into a smile. "Ah, signorina, if you would do that," she exclaimed. "I will gladly do my work and Orsola's if she can be removed from temptation. I have other daughters but they cannot come to the palazzo as servants. They are married, with families. My Orsola is a good girl. She would behave herself elsewhere. It is Angelo who is at fault." She turned then and walked briskly along the shadowy cellar corridor until we came to the iron door that led into the dry provisions room. We crossed it, and as we went through the other connecting iron door, there were approaching footsteps. It was Orsola, to tell me that Charles Voulart had arrived.

As I raced up the stone steps out of the cellars, it came to me that I'd become so involved in Matalda's distress about Orsola I'd neglected to ask her where my ball costume was. I did not turn back to ask her now. I was more interested in telling Charles about finding Dominic's things in that upstairs storeroom, which, of course, meant that I could not leave the Palazzo Rogatti, not when I was getting close to the answers I sought concerning Dominic's death.

"Now, I suppose you're all the more convinced that it was the Contessa and Angelo that Dominic hinted about in his letter when he wrote about that 'prominent Venetian family.'"

"Yes, it is the Rogatti family and not the family of that

unidentified young lady in the unfinished portrait. Perhaps not the Contessa," I amended. "She doesn't seem to have any knowledge of Dominic. Or," I added after a moment's thought, "the Contessa may be even more clever than Angelo."

"Will you please do as I ask, Teresa?" Charles said. "Leave this place. Don't let the fact that you found those articles in that storeroom turn you away from the possibility of personal danger if you remain at the palazzo. Your very life may be in danger."

I turned my face away, not wanting to give in to the tender supplication in his eyes.

"Let me stay, at least, for this evening," I said. "Angelo took it upon himself to invite the Police Inspector to the palazzo. Let me speak with him. Then I will leave."

"I will go along with that much," Charles conceded. "By the way, I wrote a couple of letters and posted them before I came here. I wrote to my mother's friend, Signora Vittoria Scalzi, asking her to come to Venice because something urgent had come up. Since she is staying with friends not far away, she'll be here soon. I'm sure Signora Scalzi will be able to tell you something about Maria Cassiano. I also wrote a brief letter to Uncle Niccolo, telling him we are coming to Vicenza to see him. I added that we may not be able to go to Vicenza immediately so, perhaps, he could come to Venice. I asked him to come to the hotel where I am staying.

"When shall I call at the palazzo this evening?" Charles asked as we rose from our chairs to leave the grand salon. "No sense attracting attention now by removing your things and Dominic's, not if you wish to speak first with the Police Inspector. When shall I stop by?"

"About nine this evening," I suggested. "And, oh, there's something else. I just remembered." I related briefly Matalda's dilemma and my impulsive promise to secure other employment for Orsola. "Matalda's worry is that Angelo would not marry Orsola if it should become necessary. I thought that perhaps you knew of someone who needed a servant and Orsola could thus be removed from Angelo—and temptation."

A wry smile passed over Charles's face. "Perhaps it is a husband, not employment, that I should seek for Orsola. Well, I will do what I can.

"Have everything packed up. Be ready to leave when I come by at nine o'clock," he said as he turned to go.

It wasn't till I left Charles and was going to my room that it occurred to me that because of Matalda's worry about Orsola I'd not only neglected to ask her about the ball costume, I'd also missed my opportunity to inquire about the locked room. Was it truly a shrine? Not to Lucia but to the child buried on the cemetery island of San Michele? There were times when I heard footsteps in the room but no chanting. It may not have always been Matalda in there.

I had become increasingly curious about that room. Now that I had formed a closer bond with Matalda, she might be the means of my gaining entry into the "shrine."

When I went to my room, I decided to begin stacking Dominic's belongings near the door so they might be easily removed when Charles returned to the palazzo later. I had no sooner begun the task when a sound from the adjoining room drew my attention. Someone was in the locked room, walking about. When I stood near the adjoining door, I could hear the soft chanting, another hymn now but the same haunting, melancholy tone. I knew immediately it was Matalda.

I knocked on the door. The murmuring chant stopped.

"It's Teresa," I said into the silent room. "I wish to speak with you."

The silence lengthened.

"I wish to speak with you," I repeated.

Slowly, the door opened and Matalda's face appeared in the narrow crack of an opening.

"I wanted to tell you," I said, "that I spoke to Charles

Voulart about looking into employment for Orsola. He promised to do so."

The tense, wary expression faded from Matalda's face. "Oh, signorina, I am so grateful to you."

"Matalda," I continued quickly, since she seemed disposed to close the door at any moment, "it was you, wasn't it, whom I have heard in this room?"

"Oh yes, signorina, it was me you heard. I often sing softly to myself. I did not disturb you, I hope."

"No, you did not disturb me." As I spoke, I tried to see past her into the room, but she held the door open only a thin crack.

"Matalda," I persisted, "why is that room kept locked?"

"Because of Fiora."

"Why is that?"

"There are clothes here, signorina, and personal articles which a guest left behind. Angelo gave me strict orders that the doors must be kept locked. He said that Fiora has been stealing some of the clothes and taking them home. She doesn't dare wear them to the palazzo because the Contessa might recognize them."

"Who was the guest?"

"I do not know. She was a guest before I came to work at the palazzo. The Contessa had been living here for a while before she employed me. Angelo said the guest intended to come for her clothes but that is no longer so. He said I might take some things home for my older daughters. The clothes will fit them because they are tall and slim. None of the clothes would fit Orsola."

"Does the Contessa also come into that room?"

Matalda thought awhile. "Lately the Contessa has done more walking about but mostly just circling the grand salon to get her exercise. This top-floor room is far away, signorina. I do not believe she comes this far. She is not well." She came to a stop, then, after a moment's hesitation, asked, "When the doctor spoke with you, signorina, did he say to you that she was—was quite ill?"

"Yes, he said she was quite ill," I answered. Not wishing to betray his confidence, I said no more.

Matalda's dark eyes misted slightly. "She is a woman of courage," she murmured. "And you, signorina, have brought her some happiness. She has told me. Yes, yes, she has said so. She told me that you have—how did she put it?—that you have lifted a great burden from her heart, that, at last, she has a purpose in life. It must be the memoirs, signorina, that she is speaking of. And she has said to me, too, that your presence has brought her a great peace."

"Speaking of the Contessa," I said, "does Angelo have the Contessa's permission to give away the guest's clothes?"

"Angelo instructed me to say nothing to the Contessa about the clothes. She does not know the guest left them behind. Angelo said there is no need to bother the Contessa about it. She sometimes worries about the smallest things. I am quite sure the Contessa has never been in this room and seen the clothes."

"What was the guest's name?" I inquired.

"I did not ask, signorina. I did not think it important."

"Matalda, may I see the clothes before you take them away?" It wasn't the clothes, of course, which interested me. Unless they would tell me something about Lucia. I also was curious about the room itself. Was Angelo partly truthful when he said it was a "shrine"?

There was a circumspect silence from Matalda, then, slowly, a smile appeared. "I see no harm in your seeing the clothes, signorina. I know that you will not steal anything." She began to ease the door open, then brought it to a stop. "Please do not tell Angelo," she said, wide-eyed. "He gave me orders that no one must come into this room."

"I will not tell Angelo," I promised.

"Then come in, signorina. But you cannot stay long. Angelo might be coming by."

The half-dark room was bare but for a trunk at one end and a dressing table at the other end. There was a wardrobe built into the wall. The double doors stood open, revealing hanging garments. It was a musty, almost empty room. I had imagined an exquisite, mysterious room, beautifully furnished—a canopied bed with fresh flowers on the bedside table.

Matalda gestured to the trunk placed against the wall. "I have almost filled it, signorina. There are still a few things in the wardrobe. Angelo will later help me carry the trunk to the gondola." She went to the wardrobe and removed a gown made of a shimmery blue satin. "Oh, my daughters will offer thanks at Sunday Mass for all these gowns. A pity Orsola is not tall and slender."

After she had lovingly placed the gown into the trunk with the others, she turned to me. "I must return now to the kitchen. I will pack up the rest later."

I was at the wardrobe, looking at the clothes there. I must get into this room again, I resolved, turning to face Matalda. She was already picking out the key from the bunch pinned to her apron. "I must lock the doors," she said. "You have seen the gowns?"

Matalda stood waiting for me to leave. I was determined to examine Lucia's clothes and personal belongings—I was convinced they were hers—and wondered at the instant how to regain entry. I went to the windows at the far side of the room. "I want to see if the Grand Canal can be seen from the window," I said as I disappeared behind the heavy curtain drawn across it.

The Grand Canal was directly below, but, more important, the latch on the window opened easily and silently. Later, when I heard Matalda's footsteps die away along the corridor, I went to the window at the end of the corridor. I unlatched it and stepped out to the loggia that decorated the front of the palazzo. The balcony led directly to the room I had just left. I entered through the unlatched window.

I went first to the wardrobe, my fingers skimming along the silky gowns which hung there. My hand came to a stop. I thought I heard a sound in the hallway. Matalda returning to finish the packing? I ran to the door and listened. All was quiet. As a precaution, I went to the door that led into the connecting bath. There was no latch. Only a key would open the door. I tried the knob. It wouldn't turn. Then, if necessary, I would have to escape through the window I had entered. I must listen intently for any sound in the corridor in order to have time to reach the window.

I returned to the wardrobe. While examining a garment hanging at the far end of the deep wardrobe, I noticed a small leather pouch on the floor. To reach it, I had to crouch down into the corner. When I emerged from the wardrobe, I froze in panic. I heard Angelo's voice in the hallway, near the door.

I was poised to make a lunge for the window at the far side of the room when the sound of a key turning and the almost simultaneous turn of the doorknob galvanized me into action. I dived under the velvet skirt that encircled the dressing table which stood near the wardrobe.

Thankfully, the room was nearly dark, or Angelo, as he entered, might have seen the movement of the velvet dressing-table skirt as I slid behind it. I wondered now whether I had carelessly left the curtain not fully drawn across the unlatched window. Had I remembered to close the window so a breeze would not stir the curtains? Charles's warning about my life being in danger skimmed through my head.

"Now, you remember our bargain, Fiora, my love," I heard Angelo say in a tender, teasing voice. "You may have two gowns of your choosing if you do what I ask you to do."

"Angelo, I will do anything for you," Fiora giggled. "Anything you ask." The next instant she was standing at the wardrobe, so close to where I crouched I could hear her excited breathing. "Angelo, whose clothes are these?" she asked as she rummaged among the garments. "Not that American's who you said was a guest of the Contessa? Not the one who is working on the memoirs?"

"No, they do not belong to her. They belong to someone who was a guest of the Contessa's long ago. But she won't be coming back for them."

"Why ever not? They are beautiful clothes."

"Don't bother your head about that. Choose the two gowns you like best."

"This one," Fiora said excitedly. She began to whirl about the room, as if dancing around with the gown held against her. "Oh, this one, Angelo," she cried as she continued to swirl and dance about the room.

"Angelo," she squealed. "There are more beautiful clothes in this trunk. Oh, I must have this green silk."

"The clothes in the trunk are for Matalda."

"For Matalda?" Fiora lashed out. "You mean for Orsola."

There was an abrupt move, as if Angelo had lunged toward Fiora. A tumbling about the floor followed with much giggling from Fiora.

"Does that answer your question about Orsola?" Angelo demanded.

"I will never again be jealous of her," Fiora said in a silky voice. Then, her voice sharpening, she demanded, "And this American guest of the Contessa? The one working on the memoirs. What is she to you?"

Angelo laughed. "You need never feel jealous of that one. But you should have no hard feelings toward her, my love, because she will make us rich."

"She will make us rich!" Fiora cried. "But, Angelo, how can that be? How can her working on the memoirs make us rich?"

"That has nothing to do with it. That is only a sham, a pretense."

"Oh, tell me, Angelo. Tell me how she will make us rich."

"I said you may have the two gowns of your choice, didn't I, *if* you do what I ask of you."

"Anything, Angelo. I will do anything you ask," Fiora said in an intense voice. "And then we can be married, Angelo?"

"Then we will be married and live like a king and queen," Angelo declared.

"Tell me what you want of me. I will do it," Fiora begged.

"This is what you must do," Angelo began. He and Fiora seemed to be still huddled together on the floor. Angelo lowered his voice. In order to hear him, I involuntarily leaned forward slightly. My shoe brushed against the leg of the dressing table, causing a faint sound.

Instantly, I heard Angelo leap to his feet.

"What is it?" Fiora cried.

"I heard a noise in here," Angelo exclaimed. "Didn't you hear it?"

CHAPTER 8

"I heard no noise," Fiora clamored. "Or it might have been a mouse in the walls. You said there were mice in the palazzo."

Quick footsteps crossed the room to the window wall. "That is what you heard," Fiora exclaimed. "There is a gondola below taking on several passengers. They are very noisy. That is what you heard.

"Go on with what you'd begun to tell me," she implored, swiftly recrossing the room. "Tell me, Angelo," she coaxed seductively. "Tell me what you want of me. You said that if I do what you ask, we will become rich and then we can be married."

"Yes, you sly little temptress," Angelo laughed. "The American young lady will make us rich. But she doesn't know that. Now this is what you must do," he continued, his voice altering to a brisk, business-like tone. "Today I will have you meet this American guest. You will engage her in conversation. She can speak Italian. Her mother was born in Venice and taught her the language. Find out all you can about her dead fiancé."

"Dead? How did he die?"

"Now why should that concern you? Listen carefully to what I say. When you meet the American young lady, ask her about her fiancé—and behave as if you were so very sorry that he died. His name, by the way, was Dominic. Find out who his friends were. He was a portrait painter but that is not the important thing. He was connected with some other business."

"What other business?"

"That need not concern you. Find out all you can about the fiancé, who his friends were, what places he visited. Ask whatever seems natural. Just be sure it all sounds friendly and natural so she won't become suspicious."

"Then I tell you what she has told me?"

"Of course. There is another person I want you to ask questions about. The fiancé's uncle. His name is Uncle Niccolo. Try to learn his whereabouts."

"I—I don't know exactly what sort of questions I should ask," Fiora broke in anxiously.

"If I thought you would fail me, you sly little devil, I wouldn't ask you to do it," Angelo answered in a tender, laughing voice. "Come to my room. I will give you further instruction. Bring with you the two gowns you've selected."

When the door closed behind them, I eased myself out from under the dressing table. After a slow, torturous straightening up, I resumed my search among the remaining garments in the wardrobe. Fearful that Fiora and Angelo might return for still another gown or that Matalda might come to finish packing the trunk, I hastily went through the pockets of a pelisse hanging in the wardrobe. I peered into a hatbox on the top shelf, then rummaged through the gowns Matalda had placed into the trunk.

I found nothing of any consequence, nothing which shed light on the mystery surrounding Lucia. I decided to leave the room before I was caught trespassing. I didn't expect to be lucky a second time, especially if Angelo should return. I went to the window to let myself out, when I remembered about the small leather pouch under the dressing table.

Returning to the window with it, I pulled open the pouch and removed a gold locket on a thin chain. Inscribed on the face of the locket were the words *To Lucia, My Love*. When I opened the locket, I gasped. The portrait inside was of me. It looked like Dominic's work. I looked closer, studying the face. It was not my face. And the gown was one I'd never owned, nor were the earrings. But the face was like mine. Was it any wonder that Angelo had stared so when he first saw me sitting in front of Florian's? I could understand now why the Contessa was startled when she first saw me—not because I resembled her deceased daughter. Because of my striking resemblance to the mysterious Lucia, she thought I *was* Lucia. There was space for a portrait facing Lucia's, but there was no portrait there.

After debating whether I should take the locket with me, I replaced it into the pouch and tossed the pouch into the wardrobe. I was quite sure Angelo on occasion searched my room. I didn't want him to find the locket and, at the moment, I saw no reason for keeping it.

I then crept out the window, ran along the loggia, and re-entered the palazzo by way of the window which I had left unlatched. Soon after I entered my room, there was a knock on the door. As I had expected, it was Fiora. Having only heard her and not seen her, I had imagined her much younger and to be as seductive as her voice, with a piquant, tantalizing face and teasing, mischievous eyes. But she was tall and rail-thin, much older than I had pictured her, no seventeen-year-old but closer to twenty-seven.

She slid into the room as she introduced herself, explaining that it was time we finally met. She glanced about the room with a quick, alert sweep of the eyes. I was glad I had had the time to replace the items from among Dominic's belongings which I had placed near the door for Charles's easy removal, or Fiora might have remarked about it to Angelo.

"Angelo, my fiancé, has frequently spoken of you," Fiora was saying as her gaze lingered on the unfinished portrait placed on an easel. "Angelo has told me that your fiancé was a portrait artist." She crossed the room to inspect the portrait. "He has also told me that your fiancé died recently," she said, turning to face me.

I sat down and gestured to the chair facing mine. "Won't

you sit down?" I said. I did not wish to shorten the visit. Perhaps I would learn more than she.

"I was so very sorry to learn of your fiancé's death," Fiora said, dropping her voice to a low murmur. She regarded me with a melancholy expression. Her eyes, I observed, were light brown like Angelo's but with yellow flecks in them. They reminded me of the yellow-eyed cats I had seen prowling about the cemetery island, the same, unblinking, straight stare, too.

Fiora had been well rehearsed during her period of instruction in Angelo's room. She moved smoothly from one group of questions to another, covering every possibility from why Dominic came to Venice to who his friends were. "Perhaps I might know some of the same people he knew," she said. She also inquired about Uncle Niccolo, explaining that Angelo had mentioned him.

The questions continued. Although I gave her no information worth repeating to Angelo, Fiora did not show impatience or disappointment. She remained cordial to the end of the visit, promising that she and I would see each other again soon so we may know each other better. "I will be coming to the palazzo more frequently," she explained, "now that the Contessa has decided to hold the San Toto Ball. Since she gave Angelo so little notice, I will be coming to help him."

"Do you already have your ball costume?" I asked in order to have something to say.

Fiora's thin, narrow face tightened. "I have not been invited. The Contessa does not consider me worthy of an invitation." The tight expression softened. She smiled. "But I hope to see you again and we'll have another friendly visit."

When Fiora left, I went down to the garden. My head was so filled with all that had occurred within the last hour or so I wished to have my attention diverted for a while. The tranquil beauty of the palazzo garden never failed to captivate me.

Immediately upon entering the garden, I felt an easing of

tension. Enclosed as it was by high stone walls, the garden was a serene refuge. The rhythmic lapping of water in the canal behind the garden wall added to the feeling of tranquillity.

I sat down in the chair under the mimosa tree, breathing in its heady scent, my eyes wandering about, from the lush purple lantana to the creamy-white oleander blossoms which trembled slightly in the soft breeze.

But I could not dismiss from my mind the conversation I had overheard. I had guessed correctly after all. It was Angelo's desire to uncover certain information about Dominic which brought me to the Palazzo Rogatti. And Uncle Niccolo was certainly connected with it. No doubt, that mysterious "business enterprise" which Dominic had never explained to me was at the bottom of it all. My resemblance to Lucia was an excuse to bring me to the palazzo. The memoirs were only a pretense, Angelo had said to Fiora. At least, resuming the memoirs had raised the Contessa's spirits and she was eager to complete them. Recalling what the doctor had told me—that she did not have long to live and knew it—I could understand why she was so determined. And Lucia? There apparently had been some animosity between Lucia and the Contessa, perhaps some misunderstanding which the Contessa now wished to set right. I knew that the Contessa was still thoroughly convinced that I was Lucia. If my voice differed from Lucia's, the Contessa's impaired hearing would not catch the difference. Her poor eyesight would cloud over any slight difference in my appearance. Furthermore, the Contessa's belief that I had been a patient for five years in a sanatorium would additionally account for any alteration in my general appearance. After seeing that face in the locket, I knew that I could easily be taken for Lucia.

It occurred to me now that the rambling which the Contessa sometimes indulged in could very well be due to medication.

The sound of a door opening drew my attention to the

house. Angelo came into the garden with a portly, uniformed officer at his side. The Police Inspector had arrived.

The Police Inspector, although affable and voluble, was unable to focus his attention on the matter at hand. Between sips of the wine which Matalda had brought to the garden he promised that yes, he would look into the circumstances of my fiancé's death and yes, he would also learn what he could about Uncle Niccolo. But his consuming interest was the Palazzo Rogatti. He was bedazzled. He could not stop exclaiming over its wonders. On his passing through the palazzo to enter the garden, he had not overlooked a single mural, not a single painting, nothing. He spoke with hushed reverence of all its marvels.

"Aah, I had heard of the Palazzo Rogatti," he said to Angelo, "and the priceless treasures within its walls. I am overcome. And the Contessa," he went on. "I have heard much about that lady."

"Would you like to meet her?" Angelo inquired.

The Police Inspector's eyes sparkled. "Is that possible? It would be such an honor. My visit would not disturb her?" he inquired timidly.

"Not at all," Angelo replied, rising from his chair. "Come, I will take you to her."

The Police Inspector flew up from his chair, belying his massive weight. "I will do all I can to seek the information you desire," he said to me over his shoulder as he trotted eagerly after Angelo.

When, shortly afterward, Angelo returned to the garden, he informed me that the Contessa and the Police Inspector took to each other immediately and were already fast friends. "I am sure the Police Inspector will be helpful," Angelo began, but was interrupted when Matalda came into the garden to inform me that Charles Voulart had arrived and wished to speak with me.

"That was a fine wine you chose, Matalda," Angelo said, beaming at her. "And it is a fine start you've made, getting the palazzo ready for the ball," he continued, but Matalda only stared at him unsmiling, then turned and went toward the house.

"What is wrong with Matalda?" Angelo muttered. "All at once she scowls at me and has little or nothing to say to me. Even now, she stands there, glaring at me."

I turned to see that Matalda had not entered the house but waited for me at the door. She must be anxious about what Charles has to say, I thought. She is hopeful that he has already secured employment for Orsola.

"It must be the frantic preparations for the San Toto Ball that have ruined Matalda's sweet disposition," Angelo said. I was tempted to tell him the reason for Matalda's gloom, but she was calling to me from the doorway. "Your friend is waiting to speak with you, signorina," she urged.

Charles was in the grand salon, our usual meeting place. "Uncle Niccolo has arrived," he said. "He'd gone to the cemetery island to inquire of the priest whether you'd come there, because he wished to get in touch with you. The priest told him where you were staying. When he hesitated, the priest gave him my address, and Uncle Niccolo came to see me. He's now in my hotel suite waiting to talk with you. I hope you can get away, because he is leaving Venice directly after he's spoken with you."

"Then I am not going to seek the Contessa's permission. Besides, she is still with the Police Inspector. He came to call. I don't expect him to be helpful, not helpful to me at least. I'm going up to my room for my reticule," I said. "I won't be long."

"By the way," Charles said, "I went to see the landlady. She said she did not bring any of Dominic's belongings to the palazzo."

"I thought as much," I said as I went toward my room.

On our way out, I informed Matalda that I would be gone for a while on some urgent business, adding that the employment situation had not yet been decided.

"What has Uncle Niccolo told you?" I asked Charles as the gondola slid away from the mooring pole.

"Nothing. That is, nothing of importance. He still has the money problem. That is what brought him to the cemetery. He's still hoping that some of Dominic's inheritance is somewhere and he can be repaid for the funeral expenses. Although he told me nothing, I hope he has some important information for you."

"Speaking of important information," I said, "I heard—no, I overheard some important information a short time ago." I told Charles of my experience in the so-called "shrine," where I was forced to hide under the dressing table. "It isn't a shrine," I said. "Only an empty room with Lucia's clothes and some personal belongings in the wall wardrobe. While I was hidden under the dressing table, I heard Angelo tell Fiora that she must help him extract information from me about Dominic and Uncle Niccolo, information which will make them rich. From the time I've been at the palazzo, Angelo has never stopped slipping in questions about Dominic and Uncle Niccolo. He's been subtle but persistent. Evidently, I'm not telling him what he wants to know, so he's enlisted Fiora's help."

We arrived at the hotel where Charles was staying. For the time being, all else fled from my mind. The sight of the palatial hotel rivaled the splendor of the Palazzo Rogatti and in some respects exceeded it. I gazed enraptured at the magnificent foyer, where marble pillars soared to a richly painted ceiling from which four Venetian glass chandeliers were suspended. Lustrous blue damask curtains were draped at high, arched windows.

"I asked Uncle Niccolo to wait in the music room of my suite," Charles said as we ascended a curved marble stairway.

I followed Charles through a foyer as luxurious as the one downstairs, only on a smaller scale. We entered a room of dark-paneled walls with a large golden harp standing at one of the windows.

A slight, courtly-looking gentleman, about sixty, with a mane of white hair and a trim, pointed white beard, sprang from his chair when we entered. He wore an elegant suit of a velvety black material. A narrow red silk neckcloth was tied into a bow beneath the short white beard. The alert dark eyes swept over me before he greeted me with a graceful, courtly bow. He then turned to Charles. "I thank you for bringing Signorina Weston here. We will not take up any more of your time. The signorina and I will have our conversation while we stroll in the Piazza San Marco," he said, taking my arm and steering me to the door.

There followed an awkward silence. I glanced from Uncle Niccolo to Charles, who, after a flurry of confusion, smiled and said, "If you wish, signor. But will you return Signorina Weston here after you've had your private conversation?"

Uncle Niccolo did not reply, only thanked Charles again for his trouble and led me out of the room.

"I do not trust that one," Uncle Niccolo muttered as we descended the marble staircase to the foyer.

"You've met him before, haven't you? He knew Dominic."

"I have met him now for the first time. I am not surprised to learn that Dominic came to associate with the likes of him. Unfortunately, Dominic would not listen to me. He soon began to associate with all sorts of questionable people. He never told me their names. He became secretive. This Frenchman whom I've just met is obviously one of those questionable people with whom Dominic had struck up a friendship."

"Why are you so displeased with him?"

"From the moment I entered his hotel suite, he proceeded to ply me with questions. I told him nothing. He has some ulterior motive." Uncle Niccolo stopped short and regarded me with a frown. "The priest at the cemetery told me that you were staying at the Palazzo Rogatti. How did you come to be a guest there?"

I explained briefly the train accident in Genoa. "I lost all my money, all my belongings. I was offered employment with the Contessa to help with her memoirs. It was her nephew, Angelo, who suggested the employment to me. I needed money for my return passage to America. There was another, even more important reason for my taking the position," I added. "I have felt all along that the Rogatti family was the 'prominent Venetian family' Dominic had mentioned in his last letter to me, the family who was going to help him with his business venture."

We had come out of the hotel and were walking along the quay toward the Piazza San Marco. I stopped and turned to face Uncle Niccolo. "Was it the Rogatti family that Dominic meant?"

Uncle Niccolo shrugged and raised his hands, palms up. "I do not know whom Dominic meant. We soon began to have our differences about business matters. He no longer confided in me."

"What was the nature of the business enterprise that Dominic wanted to pursue?"

"He didn't know himself. He would talk to me of some grandiose plans about paintings and such, some high-blown talk of import and export, but I could soon tell that Dominic had no head for business. He was a dreamer."

"And you? What business enterprise interested you?"

"What had always interested me—horses. I'd hoped that Dominic and I could associate ourselves with some acquaintances of mine and become partners in a horse-breeding farm in Padua. These acquaintances of mine had come to Venice. I learned that they were planning to return to Padua. I was eager for Dominic and myself to join them in the horse farm business. I did not have enough money but, with Dominic's inheritance, I'd hoped we could become part owners. Dominic would not listen to me. He wished to remain in Venice and was soon talking about this import-export scheme. If the Contessa Rogatti and this nephew of hers, Angelo, were the ones who were to help Dominic in this enterprise, I know nothing of that. I'd even wondered whether there wasn't something illegal about that import-export scheme.

"I do not want the Contessa or this Angelo to know of me," he declared vehemently. "That is why I did not go to the Palazzo Rogatti. I do not wish to become involved with them." He stopped, thought a moment. "I was fond of Dominic," he said in a gentle tone. "He was a fine young man. But he had no head for business. He was a good portrait painter and that is what he should have been satisfied to do. But Dominic had this foolish dream of becoming rich all at once. No, I do not want anyone at the Palazzo Rogatti to know of me."

"Then you don't know for certain who this 'prominent Venetian family' is?"

Uncle Niccolo shook his head. "It might be those people at the Palazzo Rogatti. As I've told you, Dominic became secretive, even about his association with that Charles Voulart person, who certainly must have important business connections to live in such high style.

"And I?" he added after a gloomy silence. "I must now live like a pauper. I left my employment in Padua and spent my small savings when I came to Venice. What little money I had I spent on Dominic's funeral expenses. I have now found employment in Vicenza, but it is not to my liking because it has nothing to do with horses."

We entered the Piazza San Marco and Uncle Niccolo suggested that we have a *gelato* at Florian's.

"Please try to understand," Uncle Niccolo said after he had given our order to the waiter. "I was fond of Dominic and was deeply saddened by his death, but had it not been for my brief business association with him, I would not be in such a difficult financial position. Of course, I am partly to blame," he added. "I should not have abandoned my employment in Padua."

After unburdening himself, Uncle Niccolo lapsed into a

reflective silence, eating the *gelato* which the waiter brought. "Do you know anything of Dominic's inheritance?" he inquired after a while. "The money his grandmother left him? Perhaps there is a little money left and—" His voice faltered. His face colored with embarrassment.

"I know nothing of Dominic's inheritance, but I am quite sure he brought all the money with him to Venice. His grandmother was not rich. I cannot help you. I am penniless. The Contessa is not going to pay me until the day I leave Venice. That was the arrangement and I was in no position to make demands. I was grateful to have free lodging and earn my passage money."

"You believe Dominic was somehow connected with the Palazzo Rogatti, don't you?" Uncle Niccolo said.

"Yes. In fact, I am quite sure he'd been there, if only for a short time. I found some of his belongings at the palazzo. And Angelo, the Contessa's nephew, is extremely curious about Dominic. He is constantly asking questions. By the way, he is also curious about you."

"About me?" Uncle Niccolo exclaimed. "He has no reason to be. But you must not tell anyone at the Palazzo Rogatti about me," he repeated. He leaned forward and added in a firm, emphatic tone, "And you, signorina, should leave the Palazzo Rogatti the instant you are paid your wages. Nor should you have any dealings with that Charles Voulart. Do not trust him."

"He has been kind to me. He is the only friend I have in Venice."

"He has some hidden motive," Uncle Niccolo affirmed. He rose from his chair. "Now that we have finished the *gelato*, signorina, let us stroll about the Piazza for a spell."

I remembered then about the unfinished portrait and mentioned it to Uncle Niccolo.

"The young lady, no doubt, was just another client," he replied. "If it is incomplete, it was probably the portrait Dominic was working on shortly before he died."

"Died of what?" I could not conceal my anxiety.

Uncle Niccolo regarded me with a puzzled frown. "Don't you know? You ask the question as if there'd been foul play. He died of natural causes. It was a brain hemorrhage. Isn't that what the doctor told you?"

"I went with Charles Voulart to see the doctor, but we were told the doctor went to Mantua to visit his sister."

"You went with Charles Voulart?" Uncle Niccolo said with an accusing look.

"Perhaps you dislike him only because of his French name."

"There is something about the man which puts me at odds with him. How is it that he can live in such splendor?"

"He is a banker. I believe there is wealth in the family. Also, he is not actually French but Swiss."

"Is that what he told you?" Uncle Niccolo said, and I knew by his tone of voice that I would never convince him of Charles Voulart's honesty.

Our stroll about the Piazza was brief. Uncle Niccolo explained that he had to return to Vicenza immediately. When we reached the Piazzetta, Uncle Niccolo began to walk away from the direction that led to Charles's hotel. "I am not returning you to Voulart," he said. "Have nothing more to do with him. I will escort you to the Palazzo Rogatti."

"You know where it is?"

Uncle Niccolo smiled. "Signorina, everyone knows where the Palazzo Rogatti is located."

When we were still some distance from the palazzo, Uncle Niccolo came to a stop. "We will part here," he said. "You have but a short distance to go unescorted. I do not wish to get any closer to the palazzo. I have heard of the Rogatti family. Scoundrels, all of them. Do not remain there any longer than you must.

"I am sorry our meeting had to be such a short one, Signorina Weston," he added, his voice softening. "But I must return to Vicenza. If you do not return to America immediately, come to Padua. Dominic's relatives live there. I hope to return there soon. I am confident that I will eventually secure employment there. And forgive me, signorina, for troubling you about my money problems."

Then, as if afraid that one of the "scoundrels" from the Palazzo Rogatti might accost him, Uncle Niccolo quickly executed his courtly little bow and vanished into the crowd.

As I crossed the courtyard of the palazzo, I thought back to the advice Uncle Niccolo had given me. I would do as he advised and leave the palazzo the instant I was paid. As for having nothing more to do with Charles, I had my doubts . . .

I had come to the flight of stone steps in the courtyard which led into the palazzo. I was jolted out of my preoccupation by the sight of the two stone gargoyles at the foot of the stairs. I had seen them before many times. After a while I went past them without actually seeing them. Now, as I came upon them, the gargoyles seemed larger, more grotesque. The bulging eyes stared at me, the long, lolling tongues appeared to move, the scurrilous smiles seemed to mock me.

I gave myself a shake to break the peculiar spell that had gripped me, and raced up the stairs.

Shortly after I entered my room, Orsola came to tell me that the Contessa wished to see me. She brought my ball costume, which I hung in the wardrobe.

With the words "Scoundrels, all of them" still sounding in my head, I was not eager to be with the Contessa. However, for the two hours that we worked together on the memoirs, she was so charmingly cordial that Uncle Niccolo's harsh characterization of her faded from my memory. His money problems embittered him, I decided. It was probably the sight of Charles's opulent hotel suite which had turned him against Charles, reminding him of his own circumstances.

When, later, I returned to my room, I heard Angelo's agitated voice coming through the open window from the garden below.

"I will not do it," Angelo was saying in an angry voice. "No one can make me do it."

The next voice was Charles's. "But you will do it. She will make you do it."

Unlike the previous time when I had discovered Charles and Angelo conversing in the garden I did not delay but rushed down there directly.

Angelo's face was flushed with repressed anger. His eyes gleamed hotly. Charles, smiling, turned to me. "I trust you have not yet had dinner, Signorina Weston," he said, amusement still in his voice. He glanced at Angelo, who glared at him with smoldering silence. "Signorina Weston and I will go out to have some dinner," he said, taking me by the arm.

"What was that all about?" I asked as Charles swiftly guided me out of the palazzo to the landing stage.

"I advised Angelo to let little Orsola alone," Charles replied as he helped me into a gondola. "I warned him that if he didn't, Matalda would see to it that he married Orsola. He protested, arguing that no one could make him marry Orsola. I told him that he underestimated Matalda."

"What was Angelo's decision?"

"The frightened look on his face was sufficient answer. Oh, by the way, I have been invited to the San Toto Ball. I pointed out to Angelo that my apprising him of the situation was deserving of an invitation so that you might have an escort. He promised me an invitation and a costume." He stopped abruptly, his face all at once serious and probing. "Tell me what Uncle Niccolo told you," he said.

He stared at me with disbelief when I told him that Uncle Niccolo had actually told me nothing. "Nothing I didn't already know," I said. "His reason for seeing me was, as you mentioned, his hope of being reimbursed for Dominic's funeral expenses."

"There must have been something he said that was of importance."

"He told me nothing new or, at least, very little. He said

Dominic died of natural causes, of a brain hemorrhage, to be exact. He didn't think much of the Rogatti family. He said he didn't know them personally, only by reputation."

"What else did he tell you?" Charles prodded.

"That he was in need of money and that he hoped to return to Padua—to work again on a horse farm, I presume. He'd hoped Dominic would go into partnership with him, that together they'd buy a horse-breeding farm. Dominic didn't care for the idea so, eventually, he and Uncle Niccolo went their separate ways. I, of course, asked him whether he knew the identity of the 'prominent Venetian family' with whom Dominic had associated himself, but Uncle Niccolo didn't know who they might be."

"Let's forget about Uncle Niccolo for a while," Charles said after a thoughtful silence. "Where would you like to have dinner?"

I remembered the excellent meal I had had in the garden behind the small hotel where I had stayed upon my arrival in Venice.

"The food was delicious," I insisted when Charles raised his brows at my suggestion. "I remember how good the *cannelloni* were. And the Bassano asparagus. And the yellow plums called drops of gold."

"You've convinced me," Charles said, laughing.

We were greeted warmly by the same desk clerk who was there when I had registered. It was hard to believe that was only a little more than a week ago.

"So you two have finally found each other," the desk clerk exclaimed as he escorted us to the walled garden behind the hotel.

The waiter also remembered me and smiled when I ordered the same menu I had had previously.

"I will have the same," Charles said. "The signorina has praised everything highly."

The brick-paved garden was delightfully cool and serene.

The fresh scent of the lemon trees added to the pleasantness. If only Dominic were here, I thought. If only . . .

By the time we were served our golden plums, the *gocche d'oro*, dusk had fallen on the garden. Candles, enclosed in glass sconces, were lit, bathing the garden in a soft amber light. Although Dominic kept invading my thoughts, I appreciated Charles's concern for me, his friendship. Friendship? Uncle Niccolo's warning words edged into my mind. Was it friendship or "ulterior motive," as Uncle Niccolo had suggested?

"You've become very quiet," I heard Charles say, bringing me out of my preoccupation. "Not tired, are you, Teresa? I was planning on our taking a gondola ride this evening. A nighttime ride is quite different from traveling on the canal in the daytime."

"I'm not the least tired. I would like to go."

When we left the garden restaurant it was almost dark. We meandered along the quay where lighted lamps, strung along the Grand Canal, cast colored reflections in the water. We then boarded a gondola, and the moment it slid away from the water steps, our gondolier burst into song. Soon other gondoliers joined him in the singing.

As we glided along the silky black water I soon forgot about everything but the joyful singing that rang through the balmy night air. Our gondola moved along as if in rhythm with the other gondolas that surrounded us, their movements rippling the colored reflections in the water.

Then, all at once, there were no tinted lamp reflections in the water, no more singing. Our gondola had turned into a narrow back canal. We were alone.

Charles, who had been quiet during the gondola ride, saying hardly a word, began to ask questions about Uncle Niccolo. There was an urgency about his interrogation, as if he refused to believe that Uncle Niccolo hadn't given me some meaningful information.

I found it difficult to follow Charles's questions, let alone give him some kind of answer. The desolate blackness of the narrow, twisting canal, the utter loneliness of the place, made me uneasy. I had braced my back as if prepared to ward off—what? I wasn't sure. All at once Uncle Niccolo's warning words began to drum in my head. "Do not trust him . . . He has some hidden motive." The more I tried to dismiss the disturbing words, the more tenaciously they clung. The high walls of buildings on each side of the narrow, silent waterway were oppressively close.

Charles, after his press of questions about my meeting with Uncle Niccolo, was quiet. The gondolier, after his exuberant singing a while ago, was also silent.

Stop being so foolishly fanciful, I told myself. I was letting Uncle Niccolo's brief but unsettling meeting cloud my reason. I eased into the gondola seat into a relaxed position. Yet I wasn't as relaxed as I thought. The unexpected sound of Charles's voice jolted me.

"Why was Uncle Niccolo so adamant about excluding me from the meeting with you?" he asked.

"I asked him that," I replied, hoping that my voice sounded steady and did not betray my rising apprehension. "It's because of your French name."

"Oh, is that why?" Charles said, laughing.

In the narrow waterway, with tall buildings closing in on us from both sides, his laugh sounded sinister. The echo seemed to hang and tremble in the silent darkness.

I once more had to chide myself for letting my imagination run away with me. There was nothing sinister about Charles's laughter, I assured myself. Nor should I be childishly afraid of darkness. Soon we would leave this dark deserted backwater and re-enter the lamp-lit Grand Canal where there were people about, where there was singing.

But the gondola was heading into still another lonely dark canal that snaked between high walls.

CHAPTER 9

I leaned forward and addressed the gondolier. "Please get us out of here quickly," I said, aware that my voice shook although I tried to sound calm.

Charles turned sharply to look at me. "I'm sorry, Teresa," he said. "I didn't expect you would be afraid of the back canals. You should have spoken sooner." He then ordered the gondolier to return to the Grand Canal.

I immediately felt utterly foolish. It was my meeting with Uncle Niccolo which had revived my distrust of Charles.

After the gondola returned to the Grand Canal I tried to recapture the sense of enjoyment I had felt before my absurd flight of panic, but the evening was ruined. My attempts at appearing carefree were in vain.

The following morning the Contessa sent for me immediately after breakfast. I found her, not sitting in her throne-like chair as usual, but walking about her bedroom, dressed in a flowing morning gown of lustrous mauve-colored sateen. The black hair was done differently, not in the coil of braids atop her head but arranged in a softened twirl of waves and ringlets. The pendant earrings which she favored were of pearl.

"How do you like my hair dressed in this manner?" she inquired in an animated way. "This is how I may wear it for the San Toto Ball.

"It is quite becoming," I replied.

"I will dictate the memoirs while I walk about," she said. "I have always, each day, taken only a brief stroll in the grand salon, but with the San Toto Ball only two days away, I must be prepared to greet my guests and enjoy the ball without becoming fatigued, so, lately, I have been walking about more. I can now manage stairs," she exclaimed with a triumphant smile. "With Angelo's assistance, I went down to the wine cellar this morning. I wished to see personally what the stock was."

Gesturing that I take my place at the desk, she began to dictate. She recounted previous San Toto Balls, pausing in her rapid-fire dictation only once, to tell me that Maria Cassiano had acknowledged the invitation and was looking forward to the ball.

"We will stop now," she said at last when my fingers felt stiff with cramp. She went to her bedside table and removed a gold-stamped leather coin purse. She drew out several coins and pressed them into my hand. "You have been working hard lately," she said. "Not only with the memoirs but helping Matalda, too, with the many details concerning the ball. Matalda has told me how valuable you have been. Get away from the palazzo for a carefree afternoon. Take Orsola with you as chaperone."

I thanked her and left. After eating a hasty lunch, I did not seek out Orsola. Disregarding convention, I boarded a gondola alone, giving the gondolier the address of the doctor who had attended Dominic. He might have returned by now from his visit to Mantua.

When my knock on the front door was answered, I stared in astonishment. It was the young woman in Dominic's unfinished portrait.

"Oh, signorina, so you are the American fiancée he spoke of," she said after I explained my astonishment. "Yes, he'd begun my portrait," she added, gesturing that I enter. "I am the doctor's niece," she explained. "The doctor has been visiting us in Mantua, and I returned with him to Venice. I was so sorry, signorina, to hear of your fiancé's death."

As our conversation continued, I learned that her family was not the "prominent Venetian family" Dominic had alluded to in his letters. Her family had never lived in Venice and had not known Dominic. "The landlady where your fiancé had lodgings," she explained, "became ill. The doctor, my uncle, went to see her, and happened to see some of your fiancé's paintings. I went there to have my portrait done." She hesitated before adding, "But, of course, he did not complete the portrait." She gestured that I follow her to the back of the house. "I will take you to my uncle," she said. "He is sitting in the garden."

The doctor greeted me cordially. While we sipped a cool fruit drink which the niece brought, he confirmed what Uncle Niccolo had said. Dominic's death was due to a brain hemorrhage. "He probably died instantly," the doctor said. "When I arrived at the lodging house, he was already dead."

The doctor then inquired whether I was staying with relatives in Venice. When I replied that I was staying at the Palazzo Rogatti, he immediately commented about the San Toto Ball.

"After what happened at the San Toto Ball which the Contessa gave five years ago," the doctor said after a reflective pause, "one would have thought she would never give another. Evidently, the shock has worn off."

"Did you attend the last ball?" I inquired.

"No," the doctor answered, smiling. "I did not merit an invitation but, of course, I heard about it, particularly about the Conte's death. The doctor who was called to the palazzo that evening is a dear friend of mine although I do not see him frequently. He is quite old now, confined to his sickroom much of the time."

"You know him? Is there any chance of my speaking with him?"

"If you wish, yes. I will have my niece conduct you to his house. She knows Venice well."

The niece graciously agreed to do so. While she waited downstairs in what had been at one time a waiting room for patients, the housekeeper conducted me to an upstairs room, not a musty, gloomy sickroom with a feeble patient lying in bed but a bright, sunny room with a canary chirping in a cage near the open window and a frail-looking but chipper man sitting in an armchair near the window, reading a newspaper.

He asked me to sit down in a chair near his and, after he remarked about some things he had read in the newspaper, I brought up the subject of the San Toto Ball five years ago.

"I remember it all clearly," the doctor said. "After all, it wasn't so long ago. It was all over with by the time I arrived at the palazzo. I mean about the Conte. He'd fallen down a long marble staircase and broken his neck."

"Broken his neck? He did not die of a heart seizure?"

"No, not of a heart seizure. The Contessa spread that word about Venice. He died of a broken neck. There was a strong smell of liquor on the Conte. The Contessa might have wished to prevent rumors that he'd fallen because he'd had too much to drink."

Since the doctor, to my surprise, had made no mention of it, I said, "Don't I remind you of anyone?"

The doctor leaned forward and adjusted his spectacles. It wouldn't have been his eyesight which would have prevented his seeing my resemblance to Lucia. He was reading a newspaper when I entered. His eyes appeared clear and intelligent.

"No, signorina, you do not remind me of anyone," he answered after scrutinizing my face.

I told him then of Lucia, that she had been a guest at the ball.

He shook his head. "There was no guest there named Lucia, no one who resembled you. I became quite aware of the guests, since they were detained for some time. They, of course, had removed their masks." He stopped and smiled at me. "I would have remembered such a lovely face as yours, signorina."

I described the costume Lucia wore, thinking that might evoke recollection. He shook his head again. "There was no such person there. My memory is still good, signorina. My eyes, too." He pointed to his legs, which were covered with a shawl. "It is the legs which have run out on me. But, then, I will soon be seventy-five years old. So long as I can read and remember, I do not complain." He thought a moment. "Why is that important, signorina? Whether someone at the ball five years ago resembled you?"

How to answer him briefly? I wondered. "I thought Lucia might in some way be connected with the Conte's death."

"Connected with his death? No, signorina. The truth is the Conte had too much to drink. I remember how the Contessa kept turning to her nephew several times and repeating that the Conte had died of a heart seizure. I remember the nephew well. His name was Angelo. He had the face of an angel, a beautiful face. I remember how he comforted the Contessa."

I rose to leave and thanked the doctor for letting me speak with him. He smiled, telling me not to concern myself about the Conte's death. "Not even the Contessa worries about it any more or she wouldn't be holding another San Toto Ball. The news is all over Venice that there will be another one."

When, later, I returned to the palazzo, I stood before the unfinished portrait Dominic had been working on shortly before his death. I would give her the painting; let someone finish it. The mystery concerning the young lady in the portrait was solved. And the doctor had confirmed what Uncle Niccolo had said, that Dominic's death was due to natural causes. Which meant that I had no reason to remain in Venice once the Contessa paid me my wages. At the back of my mind there still lingered the unresolved question concerning the identity of the "prominent Venetian family." Somehow, surely, that family was a vital link. But I would take Uncle Niccolo's advice: the moment I had the money for my return passage I would leave the Palazzo Rogatti.

I turned away from the portrait on the easel and went in search of Matalda. Perhaps I could assist her in some way. I could not find her but I saw Orsola in the grand salon, part of a contingent of workers, scouring and polishing the marble floor.

Orsola glared up at me with hot, smoldering eyes when I inquired about her mother. Ignoring my question, she hissed in a low, venomous voice, "You want him for yourself, don't you, signorina?"

I gaped at her, not understanding.

"Don't pretend," she continued in the low, fierce whisper. "I am speaking of Angelo."

I then recalled Charles's conversation with Angelo, advising him to let Orsola alone or face the consequence of marriage to her. "I have no interest whatsoever in Angelo," I answered, keeping my voice down, since many of the workers had abandoned their floor-scouring chore to gape at us.

"You want him for yourself," Orsola repeated in a choked voice.

"I have no interest whatsoever in Angelo," I repeated, then walked away. I was not going to pursue the subject with an attentive audience present. I would speak with Orsola later.

I found Matalda in the music room, where I joined her in cleaning the prisms of a glass chandelier. In contrast to Orsola's animosity, Matalda was beaming with smiles, informing me immediately that Charles Voulart would not have to trouble himself about securing other employment for Orsola. "My prayers to the Virgin have been answered, signorina," she exclaimed with a loud sigh. "Angelo has tired of my Orsola. He will have nothing to do with her. Oh, she is crushed but she will soon forget him. It is a miracle."

I did not divulge the nature of the "miracle." I remained with Matalda, polishing the prisms until Angelo came to tell me that the Contessa wished to work on the memoirs.

It was unusual for her to do so at that hour. The dictation of the memoirs was usually confined to the morning. But the moment I entered her room she plunged into the dictation and kept at it till quite late. As I tried to keep up with her rapid dictation, I was reminded of what her doctor had told me, that she did not have long to live and knew it. It was as if she were racing against time. The subject of the dictation was still previous San Toto Balls, but she had not yet come to the ball held five years ago.

When, at last, she dismissed me, I was totally exhausted. After a late solitary dinner in the kitchen, I was soon ready for bed.

The following morning, when Angelo joined me at the breakfast table, he informed me that the Contessa wished to work again on the memoirs as soon as I had my breakfast.

As she had the evening before, the Contessa dictated indefatigably. It was noon when she came to a stop, saying she would not need me again till late that afternoon. "We will work for a while then on the memoirs," she said. "I will want you then to wear the medieval gown you will wear at the ball. I wish to see how it looks on you." With that, she dismissed me, explaining that she and Angelo now had some details to talk over concerning the ball.

I went to eat lunch and found Charles in the kitchen. "Matalda said I may wait here," he explained. "She said you would soon be coming down to have your lunch. Only you won't be eating lunch here," he went on. "Signora Vittoria Scalzi has arrived. She's at the hotel. I hope you can come to the hotel for lunch."

I said I was free until late that afternoon and we left.

On the way to the hotel I told Charles of my visits with the two doctors. "I was surprised to hear the doctor say that Lucia was not one of the guests at the ball five years ago. I, of course, wondered whether Lucia might have fled the palazzo before the doctor arrived. I'm sure they are Lucia's clothes I'm wearing. But I have been puzzled why, if she were coming only to the ball, there were so many of her clothes in that room adjoining mine."

"Let's hope Vittoria Scalzi sheds some light on the Lucia puzzle," Charles said. "She knew all the gossip in Florence. She knew Lucia."

When I entered the suite Signora Scalzi had engaged at the hotel, she gasped when she saw me, pressing her hands against her mouth in a gesture of astonishment.

"It is incredible," she breathed. "Charles said you resembled her but—" She continued to stare at me. "It is like seeing her again."

Charles gestured that I join Signora Scalzi on the sofa. She was a middle-aged woman, plump, with white-gray hair and a youthful pink face. "While you two converse," Charles said, "I will see about lunch being sent up."

"Charles has told me," Signora Scalzi said, "that you believe it is your remarkable resemblance to Lucia which accounts for your presence at the Palazzo Rogatti."

"Yes, I believe that is so."

"And the Contessa, Charles said, truly believes you are Lucia. Of course, after seeing you, my dear, I can understand that." She regarded me silently and shook her head from side to side. "The resemblance is incredible."

"Who is this Lucia?" I asked. "And why would the Contessa want me at the palazzo?"

"I think I know the answer to that," Signora Scalzi said. "Let me tell you first a little about Lucia. You will then understand the situation better. Lucia was actually Lucy Bartlett, an American girl from Philadelphia. Her mother, dead now, was a concert pianist. She was Italian, from Florence, and had married an American. When the mother died, Lucy, as she preferred to be called then, lived with her father in Florence. When her father died, Lucy continued to live in his house.

"I met Lucy Bartlett about the time she'd secured the position with the Contessa, who was then living in Florence," Signora Scalzi continued. "The Contessa had decided to write her memoirs. Lucy was seventeen then. A lovely girl. Like you, my dear. It was about that time that Lucy began to call herself Lucia. Giovanni Tassello was the reason. You have probably heard the name. The family is a very important one in Florence. Lucia—no one called her Lucy any more—was very much in love with Giovanni. Eventually, a wedding date was set. Lucia, however, continued to help the Contessa with the memoirs." Signora Scalzi paused and raised her brows. "Then, alas, the Conte returned from one of his absences from Florence. Lucia caught his eye."

"Which, of course, made the Contessa unhappy."

"Not for the reason you might think, my dear. The Conte's wandering eye was nothing new to the Contessa. He was years younger than she and extremely attractive. The Conte's mistresses and his long absences from the Contessa were common knowledge. But the Contessa was wildly in love with the Conte. When his scandalous goings-on could not be denied, the Contessa never accused her husband, at least not publicly. She ridiculed the women who, she claimed, were making fools of themselves, much to her husband's amusement and, occasionally, his exasperation. The mistresses never lasted long. The only one who distressed the Contessa was Maria Cassiano, who was the Conte's mistress for quite some time."

Our conversation came to a temporary halt. Charles had re-entered, accompanied by three hotel servants carrying laden trays. When we were seated at the luncheon table in the dining room of the suite, Signora Scalzi resumed her conversation. "Maria Cassiano, as I was saying, was the Conte's mistress—until he saw Lucia."

"Then she became his mistress?" I asked.

"No, she did not. Lucia had eyes only for Giovanni. She was most eager to become part of Giovanni's family. She abandoned many of her American ways and was becoming quite Italian in order to please his family. She rarely spoke English any more. I'm sure she was aware that Giovanni's family had expected him to marry a certain Florentine girl, of a family as renowned as their own. The Conte's infatuation embarrassed Lucia. She was fearful that Giovanni's family might become displeased if they heard of it.

"Although Lucia scoffed at the Conte's attention, he continued to pursue her. It was Lucia's mockery of the Conte that nettled the Contessa. To the Contessa's peculiar way of thinking, Lucia's rebuffs and laugh-provoking remarks were worse than if she'd become another of his mistresses."

"Did Lucia continue to work with the Contessa on the memoirs?" Charles asked.

"For a while, yes. The Contessa was a great one for pretending a situation did not exist. Everyone talked of her being half blind and terribly hard of hearing, but she pretended it was not so. Also, the Contessa was most anxious to complete her memoirs and in that respect she was well pleased with Lucia. Later, however, Lucia left her position with the Contessa, possibly to avoid the Conte, possibly because the Contessa dismissed her. There was talk that out of vengeance the Contessa had gone to Giovanni's family. Who knows what she told them? There were those who waited for an announcement that the wedding was canceled, but that did not happen. In fact, Giovanni and Lucia were invited to the San Toto Ball. It might have been Giovanni who secured the invitation to quell the rumors, or it might have been the Conte who ordered the Contessa to invite Lucia. Maria Cassiano, the discarded mistress, was not invited."

I then told Signora Scalzi that the doctor who had been called to the palazzo the night of the ball claimed Lucia was not present.

"That isn't so," Signora Scalzi declared. "She was there. With Giovanni. He probably whisked her away just before the doctor and police officers arrived in order to avoid further gossip."

"What, then, happened to Lucia?" I inquired. "She did not marry Giovanni, did she?"

"Shortly afterward, Giovanni married the young lady his family had expected him to marry. And Lucia simply vanished. She never returned to the house in Florence. There was talk she'd gone to Switzerland, to live there. Some said she'd returned to America. I asked Maria Cassiano about

Lucia. She reminded me curtly that she had not been present at the ball. I had the funny feeling that she did know something but did not wish to discuss it."

Signora Scalzi stopped and thought a moment. "Which brings me to why the Contessa wished to see Lucia again. A rumor spread about Florence shortly before the Contessa left for Venice—that she had a fatal illness and wished to die there. She also wished to complete those memoirs. Most important of all, she probably wished to make her peace with Lucia. I'm inclined to think she had gone to Giovanni's family and maligned Lucia, thus causing Giovanni to jilt her."

"That's probably what the Contessa means when she speaks of letting bygones be bygones," Charles said to me.

"I believe Charles is right," Signora Scalzi agreed. "Even though Maria Cassiano kept a tight lip for the most part, she was particularly curious about Lucia and was constantly alert to any news about her. The talk was that it was Maria Cassiano who learned that Lucia had suffered a nervous collapse and had gone to Switzerland to stay with friends. I'm sure these rumors about Lucia's poor health got back to the Contessa. Lucia, after all, had been somewhat of an innocent victim."

"If Maria Cassiano was the Conte's most constant mistress," I said, "why is the Contessa so determined that she be a guest at the ball tomorrow? Does she want to show me off to Maria Cassiano to let her know that all is forgiven? And would Maria Cassiano also believe I am Lucia?"

"As for believing you are Lucia, yes, quite possibly. Only your voice is different. And I doubt that Lucia and Maria Cassiano ever spoke to each other. Or, for that matter, they might have never met. Oh, I'm sure Maria Cassiano saw Lucia. She couldn't resist that. Maria Cassiano was away from Florence much of the time, touring." Signora Scalzi hesitated before going on. "I doubt that the Contessa cares whether or not Maria Cassiano meets you. It's—now I don't know how true this is. I heard it said that Maria Cassiano started the story that the Conte had not died of a heart seizure but that the Contessa pushed him down those stairs."

"After such an accusation, the Contessa invites her to the ball?" I said. "And Maria Cassiano is foolish enough to accept?"

"You say that because you don't know Maria Cassiano. She possesses an insatiable curiosity. She could not resist the Contessa's invitation."

"Do you suppose the Contessa intends to harm her?" Charles inquired.

"Not in any violent manner. It might even be that knowing death is imminent, the Contessa wishes to make her peace with Maria Cassiano also."

"Considering all you've related," I said, "I'm more convinced than ever that I should not attend the ball."

"You should attend," Charles said. "Aren't you the least curious?" he added, smiling. "Don't you want to see the meeting between those two?"

"I wish I could be there to witness that meeting," Signora Scalzi declared. "Now, let us put aside all that," she added with a sweeping gesture. "Let us talk no more of Lucia and the Contessa and Maria Cassiano. I wish to talk about Teresa Weston, the lovely young American lady. Tell me something about your America, my dear. I long to go there someday." She turned, addressing Charles. "While Teresa and I chat, Charles, go and put on your costume. I wish to see it. Probably Teresa would also like to see it."

After Charles left, I remembered a question which I now put to Signora Scalzi. "If Lucia had come to Venice only to attend the ball," I asked, "why did she bring so many clothes with her?"

"Many clothes?"

"A great many."

Signora Scalzi gazed at me, bewildered. "That is strange. I—I cannot imagine why."

"Equally strange," I went on, "is why did Angelo tell me that Lucia was the Contessa's daughter?"

"Daughter? That, too, is perplexing, particularly since the Contessa could contradict him."

"She has, but Angelo wasn't present and I thought it wise not to inform him."

Signora Scalzi lapsed into a thoughtful silence, mulling over my inquiries. After a prolonged silence, she shook her head, saying, "I cannot supply any answers. But don't let it worry you. As for Angelo, he's always been like that—mischievous, full of pranks." She then turned the conversation to questions about America, which kept us occupied until Charles returned, dressed in his costume. He wore not only the mask, but a full red beard and a red wig. Not till he spoke, explaining that he was a Viking pirate, did I know it was he.

When the costume preview and luncheon ended and Charles was escorting me to the Palazzo Rogatti, I told him that Signora Scalzi could not answer my question.

"Nor can I," Charles replied, adding that Angelo was a puzzling young man and full of pranks. "But forget about that and forget about Angelo. Think of the San Toto Ball. You'll probably enjoy it. There's no reason for you to avoid the ball. Besides, I'll be the first guest to arrive and I'll never leave your side."

Shortly after I returned to the palazzo, the Contessa sent for me with the reminder that she wished to see me in my ball costume.

When I entered her room, wearing the gold-colored medieval gown and carrying the mask, the Contessa stared at me and uttered a sharp, startled sound deep in her throat.

"The gown hangs a bit loose, Lucia," she said after a sharp silence. "But that is to be expected after your long confinement in that sanatorium." Her voice was composed now; her hands no longer clutched the arms of the throne-like chair in which she sat.

"I was confined to a hospital for one week only," I said firmly.

"Is that how it seems to you, Lucia? That it was for only one week?"

"I am not Lucia," I began. "I—"

The Contessa raised her hand to stop me. "I know, my dear. You call yourself Teresa." Her eyes rested on me with a tender expression. "It is better that way, Lucia, better that you've forgotten much."

"Did Lucia attend the San Toto Ball five years ago?" I asked.

The Contessa gazed at me, a smile playing on the thin lips. "Yes, Lucia, you attended the ball. You wore that gown. You see, the amnesia has not yet left you."

"You misunderstood what Angelo told you about my amnesia. I had a slight case of amnesia after the accident. I do not have amnesia now. I am not Lucia. I was not present at the San Toto Ball five years ago. I was in America then."

"Perhaps the ball tomorrow evening will bring things back to you," the Contessa said with a gentle smile. "Speaking of the ball, I want to show you the emerald necklace and earrings which I will wear." She pointed to the bedside table. "Open that drawer. You will find a jewel cask there. Bring it to me."

I hesitated. I felt defeated. I had not shaken her conviction that I was Lucia. I crossed the room to get the jewel cask.

I drew back sharply when the Contessa lifted the lid of the silver jewel cask. Placed on top of the emeralds was a small, beautifully embellished but nevertheless lethal-looking pistol.

The Contessa smiled up at me, amused. "How can you draw away from such an exquisitely wrought object?" She picked up the pistol and fondled it. "Look at it closely," she urged, holding it up. "See how beautifully it is made. See that smooth ivory in the tiny handle? The lovely carvings in the silver." She cupped it in her hand. "It is like a pretty toy, small enough to hide easily on one's person."

"It isn't a toy. It can kill a person."

"Of course it can. It would be worthless if it could not do so." She continued to fondle the pistol. "My husband gave it to me long ago, when he gave me the emerald necklace and earrings. There was a rash of burglaries in Florence at that time. He gave me the pretty little toy to protect myself more than to safeguard the jewels. He had to be away from home frequently. I was left alone in the house. You can't depend on servants. Even now I always keep the pistol in my bedside drawer. It has been there from the day I returned to Venice."

She placed the pistol in her lap and drew out the emerald necklace. "Are they not the most exquisite, the largest emeralds you have ever seen?" she murmured. "Not like Maria Cassiano's paste jewels," she hissed. "Oh, she will burn with envy when she sees my emeralds. Just as she will burn with envy when she sees the Palazzo Rogatti."

She replaced the emeralds, then put the pistol inside the cask before closing the lid. "Put it back into the bedside drawer," she said. "For the rest of the evening go and amuse yourself," she added. "Only be sure you get to bed early so you will feel fresh and lively for the ball. I will not need you for all of tomorrow," she said as I went to the door. "I will not work on the memoirs the day of the ball."

I turned to face her. "Since you will not work on the memoirs," I said hastily before courage failed me, "could you pay me my wages now? I could then be on my way to America early tomorrow morning."

"Not attend my ball?" she said in disbelief.

"I will be of no service to you during the ball. If I could be on my way home to America even one day sooner it would be most helpful."

"Not attend my ball?" she repeated. She did not appear offended so much as confused, as if she couldn't comprehend that anyone would decline such an invitation.

I repeated my request but all she said was, "Let me know tomorrow morning how you feel about it. I am quite sure you will change your mind." She smiled at me. "It will be a memorable ball. And you will not wish to disappoint the handsome escort Angelo tells me you have acquired."

As I opened the door to leave I turned when I heard her say, "I want you to know that your coming to the palazzo has brought me great joy and comfort. Now go and amuse yourself. I may not see you until tomorrow evening."

On the way to my room I encountered Fiora. I had been meeting her frequently lately and never without the conversation soon turning to questions about Dominic and Uncle Niccolo. Her inquiries had an urgency about them. The same was true of Angelo. I had not told Angelo that I had met with Uncle Niccolo.

Fiora accompanied me to my room, hardly pausing in her stream of questions. When, at last, she left, I picked up one of Dominic's art books to read, but a vague restlessness came over me. It was not Fiora's visit which caused the disquiet: I paid little mind to her incessant quizzings. It was the ball. Why did I dread it so?

I put the book aside and went down to the garden but I did not stay long. Orsola was there, stringing up colored lanterns. I soon tired of her hostile stares and returned to my room.

When I reached the top floor, I saw that the door to the "shrine" was open.

I entered the room and looked around. It was even more barren than before. The dressing table had been removed. Matalda had taken home the trunk containing Lucia's clothes. I went to the wardrobe and opened the door. All of Lucia's clothes had been removed. I bent down to see if perhaps the small leather pouch had again escaped notice. It was gone. I was still puzzled why Lucia brought so many clothes to Venice if she came only to attend the ball.

As I left the room, I encountered Angelo in the corridor. "I presumed it was permissible to enter," I said. "The door was open."

"It is no longer a shrine, signorina," Angelo said. He extended his arms in a broad gesture, a smile lighting up his face. "Did I not tell you that you would be a comfort to the Contessa? That one day soon, the room would no longer be a shrine?

"Come," he said, turning about, "join me for dinner. I do not like to eat alone. I've sent Fiora home with a servant."

"There is something I wish you would mention to the Contessa," I said as we entered the small dining room adjoining the kitchen. While we filled our plates with the cold supper Matalda had laid out on the sideboard, I repeated the request I had made of the Contessa. "Perhaps you could convince her," I explained, "that since I will be of no use to her tomorrow, she would do me a great favor by paying me my wages this evening. The sooner I am on my way to America, the better." As I spoke I was careful not to betray my fear of the ball. I tried to sound only eager to return home.

"Your request is reasonable," Angelo replied. "I will speak to her about it. By the way, now that your stay in Venice is coming to an end, have you satisfied yourself about your fiancé's death? That, after all, was the reason for your remaining here."

I saw no harm in informing him that I had spoken with the doctor who had assured me that Dominic's death was due to natural causes.

"Now that you're satisfied on that point," Angelo said, "I can understand your wish to return home. I will speak to the Contessa on your behalf."

The following morning, the day of the San Toto Ball, I hoped that my dread of the ball would leave me and that, instead, I might even look forward to it. But that was not the case.

I remained in my room after breakfast, hoping the Contessa would send for me to tell me that she would grant my request. When I ventured out of my room to ask Matalda if I might speak with the Contessa, I was informed that she had left orders she was not to be disturbed. Angelo was not about. He had gone to attend to some details concerning the ball.

When, at last, in midafternoon, there was a knock on my door, my hopes rose. But Matalda's message was that Angelo's stepbrother had come from Mestre and wished to speak with me.

"Angelo's stepbrother?" I said, puzzled. "Why would he wish to speak with me?"

"I do not know that, signorina, but he said it is urgent. I have put him in the music room. He is there, waiting for you."

CHAPTER 10

The stepbrother looked totally unlike Angelo, tall, rail-thin, his face pale, with the look of ill health. A brief smile passed over his face when I entered the music room.

His manner of speech also differed from Angelo's exuberant, self-assured manner. "I will not take much of your time," he said in a halting, apologetic tone. "And I dare not linger lest Angelo should find me here. I have come here at this moment knowing he would be away from the palazzo for a short time." He lowered himself into a chair and rushed on breathlessly. "I manage Angelo's shop in Mestre, signorina. But my health has been deteriorating. I plan to leave the shop. I have not yet told Angelo." There was a sharp pause. His thin, pale face hardened. "It is not my poor health that causes me to leave. He has too frequently accused me of mismanagement; even theft has come into his complaints. I will no longer take his abuse. Nor do I approve of some of Angelo's schemes. Angelo had told me that a certain American lady was staying at the Palazzo Rogatti to help the Contessa with her memoirs. Soon I began to question Angelo's story. Little things he'd remark about. About your fiancé and about someone named Uncle Niccolo. Angelo told me that if I heard anyone mention the names, I should inform him.

"Inform him?" the stepbrother exclaimed, his voice rising. "Why should I? I owe Angelo nothing. I have worked for him at low wages and have been accused of mismanagement and theft. I owe Angelo nothing," he repeated, then, his voice calming down, added, "So when an astonishing development occurred in the Mestre shop recently, I did not tell Angelo. I have come, instead, to tell you."

He leaned forward in his chair, placing his hands on his knees in a tense, alert posture. It was then I noticed the ring he wore. Dominic's ring, the onyx stone carved in the shape of a lion's head.

"Where did you get that ring?" I exclaimed.

He glanced from me to the ring with a puzzled expression. "The ring, signorina? Angelo gave it to me. He had been particularly harsh with me on one occasion and to make amends he gave me the ring. Why do you inquire about the ring?"

"Because it is my fiancé's ring. Take it off, please, and look inside the band. The initials D V should be there. The initials are faint but they can be read."

"I did not think of looking for initials, signorina," he said apologetically.

He slipped off the ring and peered inside, then handed me the ring. "My eyesight is poor, signorina. I see nothing there. You look."

The faint, thin initials were there.

"Then you must have the ring," he said. "It is rightfully yours. Only do not let Angelo see it," he added with a rise of panic. "Now, to go on with what I came to tell you, signorina. Recently a gentleman came into the Mestre shop, not to make a purchase, I soon realized, but to seek information about Angelo. He wished to speak with him. He then asked me whether I knew anything of a young American portrait painter who'd come recently to Venice and died a short time ago, or whether Angelo had ever mentioned him. He knew your fiancé's name, signorina. He also inquired about that Uncle Niccolo. The gentleman was astonished when I told him that the portrait painter's fiancée had come to Venice and was staying at the Palazzo Rogatti, where Angelo lived.

"The gentleman then suggested that he would like to speak with you rather than with Angelo and without Angelo's knowledge. He asked if I could negotiate a secret meeting with you. The gentleman could not leave immediately for Venice. I knew that the day of the San Toto Ball would be your last day in Venice. Also there was the problem of my meeting first with you. It had to be done without Angelo's knowledge. I remembered that Angelo and Fiora, his fiancée, were going to see the priest the morning of the ball to have the wedding banns announced the following Sunday. So, when I arrived in Venice this morning, I watched from a distance and when I saw Angelo leave the palazzo, I came to speak with you. Only Matalda knows I am here and I trust her.

"I figured out how you may meet secretly with this gentleman," he continued exultantly. "Out of filial courtesy, Angelo gave me an invitation to the ball. I gave the invitation to the gentleman. He is tall and slender like myself. I gave him my costume and mask to wear. Angelo had not seen my costume. You will recognize the gentleman immediately. He will be wearing a monk's cowled brown robe and sandals."

"Why are you doing this?" I asked. "Why are you going to all this trouble?"

"For the money. The gentleman has already paid me well for the information I've supplied him with. If he succeeds in meeting with you, I have been promised a substantial sum of money. Now that I have decided to leave Angelo's employ, signorina, that money will be a godsend."

"What does this gentleman wish to know? What is there to know?"

"Aah, signorina, on that point he has been even more tight-lipped than Angelo. As I've told you, I soon suspected that Angelo was involved in some sort of scheme but he's been very secretive about it."

"And the Contessa? Is she, too, part of this scheme?"

"No, Angelo never gave me that impression. He revealed only that it was fortunate that the young American lady could speak Italian and that the Contessa decided to resume the memoirs."

"And Lucia? How does she fit into this—this scheme?"

He looked at me blankly. "Lucia? Angelo has never spoken of her." He rose abruptly from his chair. "I must leave now, before Angelo returns. It was a pleasure meeting you, signorina," he said as he opened the door. He was about to rush out, then turned in the doorway. "Please, signorina, do be careful about the ring. Do not let Angelo see it."

"I will be careful."

"Then good day to you," he said, then hurried away.

I stood alone in the music room, gazing at Dominic's ring in the palm of my hand. Earlier that day I was determined to avoid the ball. Now everything was changed.

It wasn't till I entered my room that it occurred to me that I had not asked the stepbrother whether Charles might be involved in Angelo's scheme. That was a hopeful sign. I was casting off the nagging, unreasonable suspicions about Charles.

Not wishing to leave Dominic's ring in my room, I tied it into a handkerchief and placed it in the pocket of my skirt. When I saw Charles I would give him the ring to keep for me. Surely Charles would come to the palazzo sometime today, before the ball. The palazzo was in the throes of last-minute preparations, and I wished to get away.

It was now past lunchtime. I went downstairs, hoping to find some food remaining on the sideboard. The food was plentiful but I wasn't hungry and decided on just coffee. Angelo entered while I was still toying with my cup of cold coffee.

"You may toast the bridegroom, Signorina Weston," he shouted, laughing. "Fiora and I will soon be married. The banns will be read at Sunday Mass."

After we drank the toast, I told Angelo that I had changed my mind about the ball and would attend.

"I am pleased that you will attend," he said in a preoccupied manner, as if his thoughts were still with Fiora. "I did mention your request to the Contessa this morning. She was saddened that you should refuse her invitation to the ball. She will be heartened when I tell her that you have changed your mind.

"I must leave you now," he said as he drained his glass of wine. "I should not have eaten so fast, but I have many things to attend to."

When he left I lingered at the table, not knowing how to amuse myself for the rest of the day. I did not want to seclude myself in my room, yet I wished to escape the turmoil of the preparations.

As I was leaving the dining room I glanced out the ground-floor window to see Charles enter the courtyard. I ran to him.

"I've come to rescue you from all this bedlam," he said. "Can you get away?"

"Yes, I'm sure I can. I'll check with Angelo or Matalda."

I found Angelo in the grand salon, supervising the arrangement of potted hibiscus and oleander. He assured me that I would not be needed. "Just be back at the palazzo in time for the ball," he said as I hurried back to Charles.

"So today is to be your last day at the Palazzo Rogatti," Charles said as the gondola glided across the water toward St. Mark's. "And quite a send-off, being a guest at the San Toto Ball. I'm glad you had that talk with Vittoria Scalzi. It put to rest your hesitation to attend the ball."

"No, not quite. After I returned to the palazzo and recollected what Signora Scalzi had said, my doubts began to return. Then I had a rather disturbing visit with the Contessa and that increased my doubts about the ball to the point of my requesting that she pay me my wages now so I could leave the palazzo immediately."

"You made such a request? Did the Contessa refuse?"

"I believe she would have granted it, but, shortly afterward, I had a surprise visitor." I then told Charles of my meeting with Angelo's stepbrother. I also gave him Dominic's ring to keep for me.

"Then it is imperative that you attend the ball," Charles said. "This man the stepbrother described may be the very person that you should speak with."

I became silent, then said haltingly, "I—I know you're going to say I'm being indecisive and—and suspicious but, well, do you suppose this meeting with a mysterious gentleman is only a ruse?"

Charles placed my hand firmly in his. "Teresa, stop indulging in all those suspicions. You've been like that from the day you arrived in Venice. I can appreciate the fact that your circumstances lend themselves to such thoughts but—" He smiled. "You should speak with this man. And you should attend the ball. Don't worry about anything. I'll never leave your side. Now let's forget all about the Palazzo Rogatti," he said, sitting erect in the gondola once more. "Let's enjoy ourselves, roaming about Venice. Would you like to see St. Mark's again?"

I said I would and we went there first.

"I'm surprised I should feel the same sense of awe and mystery as I did the first time," I said to Charles as we entered the church.

"That's how I feel each time I come here."

We came to the San Clemente chapel, ablaze with blue, white, and gold mosaics. "It's the mosaics that catch my attention," I said.

"The mosaics are contrived to catch your eye," Charles explained. "They're purposely set at slightly different angles in order to catch the light. Now let's go take a look at the Pala d'Oro," he said. "It's rather unusual and has quite a history."

We entered an area behind the high altar where the large gold and enamel altarpiece was displayed.

"Tell me something about it," I said.

"The first one was made in Constantinople in 976. Then more gold panels were added. In the thirteenth century it was enlarged again, with enamel looted from Constantinople added to it. In 1345 the altarpiece was placed in its present Gothic frame.

"Let's move along," Charles urged. "There's a lot more of Venice that I want you to see. We'll go now to the courtyard of the Doges' Palace. After that, we'll go to the Merceria."

As we approached the Doges' Palace at the corner of the Piazza, I thought how frivolous the long row of lacy arcades of the palace appeared. The fringe of arcades created the illusion of sheer decoration, yet they were actually the masonry supports for the huge structure. The upper walls, too, of a creamy pink facing, seemed airy-light, as if they needed no substantial support.

"We have time for only a glimpse," Charles said as we entered the large Renaissance-style courtyard, where an imposing staircase led into the palace. "That is where the Doges were crowned," he said. "At that staircase."

The courtyard, with its many tropic plantings, was deserted. Two nuns, heads bowed as they said their rosaries, were the only other persons present. The unexpected hush of the courtyard was a welcome interlude after the throng in the Piazza and in the church.

"The Merceria won't be quite that quiet," Charles said as we left the courtyard and re-entered the Piazza. We crossed it and went through the Clock Tower arch into the crowded, bustling twist of streets lined with shops. Silks, velvets, and damasks flapped in the breeze near the doors of fabric shops. Murano glass sparkled in sunny shopwindows. Above the steady roll of the liquid Venetian language heard on all sides, the clear song of a nightingale skimmed through the air. We were approaching a shop which sold birds. A large assortment of ornamental cages was strung across the front of the shop. All the birds twittered and cooed, but the nightingale's song filled the crowded street of shops.

"It isn't just the sights and sounds," I said. "It's the various smells—the smell of leather, the tantalizing scents wafting out of the perfume shops. Which reminds me—one of the most pleasant memories I'll have of the Palazzo Rogatti is the scent of the mimosa tree in the garden."

"You like the mimosa fragrance?"

"Yes, very much."

"This way," Charles said as he drew me into still another street of shops, the Calle Larga San Marco.

I peered into the curved window of a chemist's shop where huge mysterious bottles of colored elixirs stood on glass shelves. Charles took my arm and led me into a shop a short distance away, a perfume shop where he bought me a beautifully designed bottle of mimosa perfume. "Wear it tonight to the ball," he said as we came out of the shop.

I thanked him for the gift, then asked whether we were now returning to the Palazzo Rogatti.

"Not at all. Much too early for the ball. We're going to have something to eat. I know the very place. We'll board a gondola at the Piazzetta."

The gondola brought us to a narrow, winding street which opened onto a campo. A busy fruit market displayed juicy red watermelon, rosy peaches, and large, dark purple plums.

"We'll come to the fruit market last," Charles said as we went toward a fragrant bakeshop. There we purchased a small loaf of still warm bread, then we crossed the campo to a cookshop where Charles bought some roasted chicken, a mound of rigatoni, and two ripe tomatoes. After purchasing our bottle of wine, we placed our feast on a table beside a wall to which scarlet bougainvillaea clung. A wide opening in the row of terra-cotta houses at the far side of the campo offered a spectacular view of the Grand Canal.

We ate the delicious food in a relaxed, unhurried manner, lingering over the cool, red-ripe watermelon.

After our leisurely meal, we decided to walk to the Palazzo Rogatti. We ambled along the twisting, narrow little streets and alleyways. We paused at the many humped bridges we crossed so that we might get a sweeping view of the Grand Canal. A mist had fallen on Venice, veiling the canals and alleyways with an opalescent shimmer. The pearly mist, mingling with the waning light, cast a strangeness upon the place, making it all seem unreal.

When, eventually, we reached the Palazzo Rogatti and Charles asked whether I still had any doubts about attending the ball, I was able to answer without hesitation that I had no qualms about it.

"Wear the mimosa perfume," he reminded me as he turned to leave. "And don't worry about anything. I'll be the first guest to arrive and I'll never leave your side."

CHAPTER 11

The moment I entered the palazzo courtyard, I saw that all was in readiness there to welcome the guests. When they alighted from the gondolas, they would first pass through the courtyard, then ascend the stone stairs to the grand salon, where the Contessa would greet them.

Colored lanterns were already lighted in the long, narrow courtyard, bathing it in a festive glow.

For only a moment did the sense of anticipation and gaiety leave me. It was when I approached the stone stairs to enter the palazzo. My glance brushed across the gargoyles at the foot of the stairs. The red and green lights from nearby hanging lanterns made the gargoyles' faces more sinister than ever.

I turned away from the hideous, mocking faces and ran up the stairs.

"Signorina Weston," Angelo cried when I entered the grand salon. "Oh, how you have caused me to worry! Where have you been? No, no, it does not matter so long as you have finally arrived."

Going toward the stairs, I glanced about me. The grand salon had been transformed to glittery splendor. Already, the numerous candles in the huge Venetian glass chandelier were lighted. Flowering shrubs in huge porcelain tubs were placed about the gleaming marble floor. Carnations and lilies in crystal vases were everywhere, their scents mingling.

I clutched my small bottle of mimosa perfume to me and raced up the back stairs to my room. Matalda and two serving girls soon followed me, bringing hot water for my bath.

I bathed and dressed, pleased with the way the medieval

costume suited me. I took a considerable amount of time arranging my hair, then, after dabbing the mimosa perfume behind my ears and on my wrists, I snatched up my mask and went downstairs.

I peeked into the grand salon. The musicians were already seated on the dais. No guests had arrived yet. Servants in ornate livery stood at attention. There was a feeling of anticipation in the air.

I went into the garden. The colored lanterns were strung like a canopy, bathing the garden in a fantasy of lights. The scent of the mimosa tree filled the air. I sat down in one of the many wicker chairs, deciding to wait there until the ball began.

Before long I heard voices within the palazzo. The musicians began to play a Mozart divertimento. I put on my mask and went inside. Charles said he would be the first to arrive.

There were already many costumed and masked guests in the grand salon, moving slowly from the entrance to where the Contessa stood, greeting each guest. As the hostess, she was not in costume, nor was she masked. She wore a gown of deep green chiffon with an underskirt of lighter green. The emerald necklace gleamed at her throat. The glossy black hair was swept up into a topknot of soft curls. The long pendant emerald earrings dangled from her ears. She appeared animated as she greeted her guests, pressing their hands between hers, smiling into their faces.

My eyes left the Contessa to search for Charles, a red-wigged pirate with a red beard. But I could not see him.

I returned to the garden, thinking he might have gone there to look for me. But he wasn't there, either. Re-entering the grand salon, I sat down in one of the gilt chairs near the place where still more guests were arriving, handing their invitations to a liveried servant. I kept reassuring myself that Charles was only momentarily detained. He would surely recognize me when he entered the grand salon. I had shown him my costume.

After a while I rose from my chair and walked among the guests, searching for Charles. I listened to the musicians playing a waltz; I admired the costumes of the guests, anything to prevent worrying about Charles's absence.

Turning to retrace my steps to where the guests entered the salon, I heard the Contessa address me.

"You look lovely, my dear," she said, extending her hands to me. Her eyes appraised my gown. "The medieval look suits you." She was about to continue speaking when she came to a stop and looked past me. "There is Maria Cassiano," she said. "I would know her anywhere. No costume or mask can disguise her from me."

I began to turn around to have a look at Maria Cassiano, but the Contessa placed her hands firmly on my shoulders. "No, don't turn around," she said. "I want it to be a surprise."

I barely heard her words, for at that instant my attention was drawn to a red-wigged pirate with a red beard, shouldering his way through the crowd. "There's Charles," I said aloud. I began to move away, but the Contessa still held me firmly by the shoulders. At the same instant, behind me, I heard a voice greet the Contessa. An animated conversation followed between the Contessa and Maria Cassiano, first a warm greeting, then Maria Cassiano remarking about the Palazzo Rogatti. "It is all so beautiful," she exclaimed, "simply beautiful."

I did not turn around to look at Maria Cassiano. The Contessa still held me firmly by the shoulders and, furthermore, my eyes were following Charles as he hurried toward the rear of the grand salon.

"And now, my dear Maria," I heard the Contessa say, "I want you to meet my guest of honor." I was still turned away, my eyes on Charles as he disappeared beyond the grand salon. I felt the Contessa press my arm, then say, "Remove your mask, Lucia."

"Lucia?" I heard Maria Cassiano say as I slipped off the mask and turned around.

Maria Cassiano's eyes behind the mask were wide and staring. Her mouth remained open in a spasm of shocked surprise, then she said again, "Lucia?"

I was only half aware of what was going on. My mind was still on Charles, but I recovered from my preoccupation and was about to correct the Contessa's mental lapse, but at that moment a servant appeared to tell me that someone wished to speak with me and he would direct me to the person. That would be the gentleman from Mestre. Everything else fled from my mind. I pulled away from the Contessa and followed the servant. My pulse began to race. What would the man tell me about Dominic? Would this be the information I had been seeking?

I followed the servant up the back stairs to the top floor and soon learned that he was conducting me to the room which Angelo had once called the "shrine."

"In there, signorina," the servant said, then turned and disappeared down the corridor.

I hesitated, then slowly approached the room. Why should I be apprehensive, I told myself, simply because the secret meeting would be held in that room?

The door to the room was open. When I came to the doorway, I stared in surprise. Sitting in a chair at the far side of the room was Charles, dressed in his costume, wearing the red wig, red beard, and the mask.

"What are you doing here?" I asked in confusion as I approached him.

When I reached him, he whirled out of his chair. In one swift, brutal movement he tied a thick cloth around my mouth. I tried to cry out, but no sound came through the thick cloth.

I began to flail my arms and was poised to run, but

Charles's hands snatched both my arms. He flung them behind my back and bound them securely.

"Good. You work swiftly," I heard Angelo say behind me. The next instant Charles pulled a blindfold across my eyes. "Here's the rope," Angelo said. "Tie her ankles together."

CHAPTER 12

"Place her against that wall while I lock the door," Angelo said to Charles.

I was roughly dragged across the room and pushed into a sitting position against the wall. The bindings around my wrists were so tight they cut into the flesh.

It wasn't only the terror of what was to become of me but that Charles should have deceived me so totally. No, not totally. I thought back to my initial distrust of him. Uncle Niccolo had had that same reaction.

So all of Charles's helpfulness had been only a means to an end. How diligently he had persuaded me to attend the ball, when every instinct told me that I should not, not even after the visit from Angelo's stepbrother . . .

"I wanted you blindfolded and gagged, signorina, so you do not in any way interfere with what I wish to tell you." It was Angelo's voice. It came from across the room. But someone was standing beside me. I next heard the scrape of a chair being dragged against the hard floor to a spot near me and the person—Charles, of course—sank into it.

Now that the shock of my abduction had abated slightly, I began to reconsider what had occurred during that brief moment of terror when Charles had swiftly tied the gag over my mouth. Why did I immediately assume it was Charles? The bulky costume and the red wig and beard were a perfect disguise for anyone.

Fiora, I thought. It was Fiora, not Charles. It was she who had assured Angelo in this very room that she would "do anything" for Angelo . . .

I was startled by the sound of Angelo's voice. "I'm sure you've wondered, Signorina Weston, why I brought you to the Palazzo Rogatti. That business of the memoirs never sounded convincing, but I felt it would do for the short time you would be here. You see, signorina, the original plan was that you would be killed the day you were brought to the palazzo."

I must have visibly cringed at the words. Angelo quickly said, "I see that you react with disbelief at the news. But I'd never expected you to be a guest for two whole weeks.

"For two weeks I had to keep up the charade," Angelo wailed. "The Contessa kept complicating things for me. And you, too, signorina," he complained petulantly.

A silence followed. The room became unnervingly still, yet I was acutely aware of the person near me. I no longer believed it was Charles. And if it wasn't Fiora, then who? Angelo's stepbrother? Had he lied to me? Still another part of Angelo's "plan"? In my eagerness to clear Charles of any blame, I even wondered whether it might be Uncle Niccolo who had donned the costume and the wig and beard. No, I remembered that my abductor was tall, and Uncle Niccolo was short. But Fiora was tall.

"Yes, you kept complicating things for me," Angelo repeated. "There will be no more complications from you. That is your friend, Charles Voulart, who is sitting near you. If you should make some foolish move, he will know what to do."

I could hear my strangled gasp through the gag across my mouth. I closed my eyes behind the blindfold, an involuntary response, as if to shut out the terrible truth.

There was a low laugh from the far side of the room. "Nevertheless, despite the complications," Angelo said, "the plan is an ultimate success. She will soon be here."

She? Was he speaking of the Contessa?

On the fringe of that thought I recalled the conversation I had overheard in this very room, when Angelo had assured Fiora that I would make them rich . . .

It occurred to me now that in the horror of the last few

minutes I had forgotten about the gentleman from Mestre. What had happened to him? Had Angelo and Charles somehow learned about him? Well, of course, I had told Charles about him. Or had I been correct about my suspicion that the gentleman from Mestre was only a ruse to assure my presence at the ball?

"The Contessa will soon arrive with the pistol," Angelo said with such suddenness that I shuddered. "Oh, don't appear surprised, signorina," Angelo went on. "I'm sure you've been puzzled about this Lucia thing, particularly after you'd seen the child's grave in the cemetery and knew that Lucia was not the Contessa's daughter. You did return to the cemetery, did you not? If the Contessa had not called you Lucia on that first meeting, I wouldn't have had to make up that story about your resemblance to her deceased daughter. Even so, I did not foresee a problem. I was expecting you to be killed and out of the way that same day.

"I'd warned the Contessa not to call you Lucia," Angelo grumbled. "I'd warned her that you'd been in a sanatorium for the mentally disturbed for five years and that you might become violent if the name Lucia broke through your amnesia, or that you might escape from the palazzo. Still, the Contessa either forgot herself or could not resist calling you Lucia.

"If the Contessa had stuck to the original plan and used that pistol of hers on you the day you arrived at the Palazzo Rogatti," Angelo resumed after a short silence, "I wouldn't have had to take you to the cemetery island and rush you out of there so you wouldn't go wandering about and discover the Rogatti burial ground. Oh, what a fool I'd been to jump to the conclusion that your fiancé was buried in Padua. If I'd known he was buried in Venice, I would never have spun out that story of the Contessa's deceased daughter."

Angelo lapsed into another silence, which was all the more nightmarish since I could see nothing. Why hasn't Charles spoken? I thought irrelevantly. Angelo had not addressed him, nor had Charles spoken to Angelo. And if Angelo had lied and it was Fiora who sat near me, wouldn't they have exchanged words? A new dread assailed me. Who was it who sat so quietly beside me? Who perhaps did not wish the voice to be recognized by me?

"But the cemetery island was only one of my problems," Angelo resumed. "It wasn't easy for me, signorina, especially when the Contessa decided that you would remain at the palazzo for two whole weeks. At first it was only to be a brief delay. I couldn't kill you. I could not do such a terrible thing. It is the fifth commandment, Signorina Weston. Besides, it was agreed from the first that the Contessa wished to have that privilege. So, when the Contessa insisted that you remain at the palazzo, I decided to work hard at making you believe that the reason for your being lured to the palazzo was because of your fiancé. I even drew Uncle Niccolo's name into it. It was you, signorina, who gave me the idea. You kept asking me whether I'd known Dominic or Uncle Niccolo. You appeared disbelieving when I assured you I had no knowledge of either gentleman.

"There was my opportunity," Angelo declared. "I then proceeded to convince you that I had known your fiancé and was eager to extract some information from you about him."

And he had succeeded. I thought back to the many times I was on the verge of escaping from the palazzo, only to remain because Angelo succeeded in making me believe that Dominic had been associated with the Rogatti family. I thought back to the times I had suggested to Charles that I boldly confront Angelo, tell him that I had seen the child's grave, tell him that I was aware of other deceptions; but each time Charles warned me that I would then not only endanger myself but that I would forfeit any further opportunity to unravel the mystery concerning Dominic.

If Angelo was telling the truth about Charles's complicity, how cleverly Charles had done his part, persuading me to remain at the palazzo, taking a different view—that I should leave—only when he knew that because of some newly contrived development I would choose to remain.

Charles's most astute planning was staging my meeting with Vittoria Scalzi. No wonder she had arrived in Venice so quickly. She had been no more than some Venetian opportunist whom Charles had hired to say all the right things, to make certain that I attended the San Toto Ball, since the ball was for some reason to be the most important part of the plan.

"I put those articles belonging to your fiancé in that storeroom," Angelo explained. "I expected you to find them when you were searching for the ball mask. I'd bought those things—the patron saint figurine, the book, the portrait—from Dominic's landlady. I got to her before you. It was easy to learn the address. I found a letter from Dominic in your reticule, which you'd left in your room. Oh yes, I constantly kept after you, asking you questions about your fiancé and about Uncle Niccolo. I even got Fiora to do the same. I had to make sure you had a vital reason to remain at the Palazzo Rogatti.

"No, your fiancé had nothing to do with this," Angelo drawled. "It is because of Lucia that you are here. Because of your striking resemblance to her. It was not difficult to deceive the Contessa. I remember how I myself was stunned when I first saw you in the Piazza San Marco. I knew then that my search for Lucia had ended. The likeness was miraculous."

I recalled the locket I had found in the wardrobe of this room. I, too, had been stunned at the resemblance. I remembered, too, how the Contessa had gasped when she first saw me.

Yet, even before I had seen the child's grave I doubted that Lucia was the Contessa's daughter. Too often, particularly when she called me Lucia, the Contessa's lips would twist into a secret, venomous smile. The hooded eyes would sometimes regard me with repressed hatred. When her puzzling behavior became alarming and I would consider escaping, the Contessa would abruptly become friendly and I would console myself with the argument that seeing me reminded her painfully of her daughter's insistence upon marrying someone not of her choice. Or I would conjecture that the Contessa hated herself for having caused her daughter's death. I always found some excuse to remain so that I could pursue my quest concerning Dominic and his death.

"I had the Contessa's impaired eyesight in my favor," Angelo was saying, "and her poor hearing. I began to worry just a little about the impersonation, when the Contessa changed her plan and decided not to use the pistol the day you arrived at the palazzo. When she told me that she expected you to remain for two weeks, I protested. How was I to continue the impersonation for two whole weeks? When she further complicated things by deciding to hold a San Toto Ball, I truly became upset. But she was adamant. She insisted it was only fitting that you should die the night of the ball, just as the Conte had died. Believe me, signorina, if it had not been for the generous sum of money she promised me in addition to the amount she'd agreed to initially for finding Lucia and bringing her to the palazzo, I would not have agreed to this madness about the ball. But it will soon be over with. I will be paid handsomely for my troubles. Fiora and I will then get married and live like a king and queen."

Angelo stopped speaking. The room became not only disconcertingly still but unbearably hot. The seizure of chills which had gripped me a while ago altered now to a feverish, suffocating discomfort. As an added cruelty, I became aware of the mimosa perfume I had dabbed behind my ears and on my wrists before going down to the ballroom, the perfume which Charles had bought me a short time ago in the narrow streets of the Merceria.

The utter silence in the room was broken when, through the windows, which were closed, no doubt, I heard the musicians in the grand salon resume playing.

My head ached. I pressed it against the wall, trying to dislodge the blindfold which was aggravating the throbbing pain. To my astonishment, the blindfold moved slightly. While Angelo talked, I began to maneuver my head up and down, slowly pulling away at the blindfold, careful not to draw attention to what I was doing.

"It all began with the San Toto Ball five years ago," Angelo was relating. "The Conte lured Lucia to this room to seduce her. Lucia was a young American lady, like you, signorina, living in Florence. Lucia had come to the ball with her fiancé, Giovanni Tassello, eldest son of that illustrious Florentine family. The Conte had deceived Lucia, telling her that Giovanni had become ill and was asking for her. She frantically followed him up the back stairs. When Lucia realized the Conte had tricked her, there was a struggle at the top of the stairs. The Conte fell down the marble staircase and broke his neck. Lucia rushed to tell me what had happened. When I returned to the scene with Lucia and the Contessa, it was the Contessa who expeditiously fabricated the story that the Conte had had a heart seizure. The stairway to this room, and your own next door, you know, is a secluded back stairway, so there were no guests to witness what had happened. Lucia was immediately spirited away by her fiancé, Giovanni. He did not wish to have any scandal attached to his noble name."

So that was why the doctor I had spoken with, the one who was called to the palazzo that evening, did not see anyone there who resembled me. Lucia had already gone.

"The irony of it all, signorina, is that the Conte had never failed to attract women. He was a handsome rogue, much younger than the Contessa," Angelo said, bringing to mind the portrait that hung above the Contessa's bed. A handsome rogue, indeed. I remembered the rakish smile on the attractive face.

"There'd been a long list of mistresses," Angelo went on. "But Lucia would have nothing to do with the Conte. Yet, even though she scoffed at him, the Conte pursued Lucia relentlessly. It was as if all the other women had meant nothing to him. So, the night of the ball the Conte must have realized it was his last chance. He lured Lucia to this room. And all it got him was a broken neck. To the Contessa, of course, Lucia had caused his death.

"The day of the Conte's funeral—" Angelo said, then came to a stop. The next instant he lunged toward me. At the same time I saw Charles spring out of a nearby chair. The cause of the commotion was that I'd managed to dislodge the blindfold. It had slipped down my face.

I stared into Charles's face. Because of the wig and the full beard, all I could see of his face were his eyes. He had removed his mask. I continued to stare at his eyes. They were not Charles's eyes. Angelo became aware of my fixed stare at the costumed figure's face. He snatched the blindfold, pulling it up over my head, and threw it on the floor. His eyes blazed with exasperation. "It does not matter that she can see," he muttered. "If the blindfold were not removed now, the Contessa would have ordered it removed." He turned to his accomplice. "You may as well remove that wig and beard. I know you're uncomfortable in them. The signorina already knows you are not Charles Voulart." Turning to me, he said with a shrug, "It is my stepbrother, signorina, as you have probably already guessed. He did not want you to know that he was helping me with my plan. He wished to remain disguised. He didn't want you to recognize him. Besides, you fool," he added, addressing the stepbrother, "what if the signorina does know it was you? She'll be dead in a short time."

The stepbrother removed the wig and beard and returned to his chair; he sat down, then rose and moved the chair sideways so I could not look into his face.

For the moment I forgot about my present discomfort and the terror which was to follow. My thoughts turned to Charles. What had they done to him? Killed him?

"I see that you appear particularly disturbed, signorina,"

Angelo said. "You perhaps are wondering what has happened to that nuisance, Charles Voulart? The Contessa, you see, would not honor my stepbrother with an invitation to the ball and I needed him here. He'd already done a first-class job this morning, weaving that tale about a gentleman coming here from Mestre to tell you something important about your fiancé. So, since my stepbrother had neither invitation to the ball nor costume, we persuaded Charles Voulart to relinquish his. Besides, we did not wish his presence at the ball. I will say this for him, he put up a good fight. Do you not agree?" he inquired of his stepbrother, who nodded in agreement.

I closed my eyes. An icy chill washed over me. Charles was already dead, perhaps as I soon would be. I opened my eyes when I heard a clatter. It was the stepbrother. He was moving his chair to the far side of the room, near Angelo. Once seated, he gazed out the window. Angelo was lounging in his chair, gazing at the painted ceiling, waiting. Waiting for the Contessa to appear with her pistol. How disturbed I had become earlier that day when I had first seen that pistol . . . "How can you draw away from such an exquisitely wrought object?" the Contessa had chided me when she took it out of the jewel cask. "It is like a pretty toy, small enough to hide easily on one's person," she had said as she fondled it.

"Do not concern yourself about Charles Voulart," Angelo said, drawing his eyes to me. "Let me finish my tale of Lucia. As I'd begun to say a while ago, the day of the Conte's funeral, the Contessa said to me, 'Find Lucia. I will pay you well. Bring her to me. I will do the rest.'

"Find her?" Angelo exclaimed, his eyes widening. "Signorina Weston, for close to five years I searched for her. She vanished into thin air. Giovanni would tell me nothing. He'd married a young lady of a Florentine family as renowned as his own. No taint of scandal was going to touch his family or the one into which he'd married. Nevertheless, I felt sure that eventually I'd find her and when I did, I was confident I'd be able to persuade her to meet with the Contessa. Lucia was simple and childish, as are all American girls. I knew I'd be able to convince her that the Contessa wished to meet with her so that they might become friends again and that the Contessa wished to continue with the memoirs.

"Of course, if Lucia had refused to meet with the Contessa," Angelo added with a shrug, "she would have encountered the Contessa unexpectedly. And the Contessa would have her lovely little pistol with her."

Angelo paused, staring into space. The soft cherubic contours of his face hardened. The eyes narrowed. "After a five-year hunt," he said between his teeth, "I located Lucia in a Swiss sanatorium, only to be told that she'd died there the previous month. Of a lung lesion. Had no will to live, the nun said. Not because of the Conte incident but because Giovanni had abandoned her.

"You can imagine how I felt, signorina," Angelo wailed. "All that money the Contessa had promised me blown to the winds. She'd been paying me a pittance while I continued my search but the prize money would not come to me if I did not deliver Lucia to her. I already knew that the Contessa was leaving me nothing in her will. Her reason, she said, was that she'd already given me much, including a first-class education. So, after I learned that Lucia was dead, I was determined to get the money the Contessa had promised me. I pretended to be still searching for Lucia, but I knew I would soon be told to stop. The Contessa would tire of paying me. I began to perfect my plan. I searched everywhere for someone who resembled Lucia."

Angelo stopped; he gazed at me with a triumphant smile. His eyes shimmered with a glitter of cupidity. "Then, Signorina Weston, I found you in the Piazza San Marco," he murmured. "Do you remember our little conversation at the San Giacomo di Rialto church? When I said I'd made a novena there? I made no novena but meeting you was more than an answer to a novena prayer. It was a miracle."

He thought a moment, then laughed to himself. "Do you

remember my telling you that someday I would mount the steps of the Gobbo di Rialto and make my announcement to all the people in the campo? Tell them I have accomplished what I'd set out to do?" He nodded and smiled, that engaging seraphic smile that came so easily to his face. "Tomorrow morning I will go to the campo and make my announcement.

"How well everything worked out after all," he said, emitting a sigh. "Lucia had no family, only some relatives who fought over her possessions, including the house in Florence. It was from one of those greedy relatives who established residence in the Florence house that I was able to purchase her clothes and some personal belongings, like that leather notebook she'd used when she was working with the Contessa on the memoirs. How useful the clothes and the notebook became. The Contessa didn't know I'd purchased Lucia's things, I kept them hidden in the locked room adjoining yours, the very room you're in now, the so-called 'shrine.' The Contessa did not have a key to this room. Besides, she never ventured to the top floor. Until shortly before the ball, she rarely left her room.

"It has all turned out happily, hasn't it?" he said to the stepbrother, who nodded and grinned.

Returning his attention to me, Angelo said, "I was always afraid that one day the Contessa might wake up to the fact that you were not Lucia. I was confident that deceit would hold for the space of a day, but two weeks was a different matter." He smiled. "The Contessa is still convinced you are the young lady who caused the Conte's death." He stretched his legs out before him and gazed at the tips of his shoes. "Soon it will all come to an end and I will get my promised money. I will pay you for your little service this morning," he told his stepbrother, "and for helping me with this evening's part of the plan."

Angelo was about to continue speaking but he stopped short and leaned forward in his chair. I, too, heard the footsteps in the corridor. I prayed it would be Charles, that they had not killed him.

"Here she comes," Angelo said, going to the door and unlocking it.

The Contessa entered. She came to a halt inside the door and gazed at me from across the room.

Angelo, after locking the door, sauntered back to his chair.

The Contessa slowly crossed the room halfway. She looked from me to the stepbrother, who was now sitting tense and erect in his chair, his eyes on the Contessa.

"What is he doing here?" the Contessa demanded. "I did not invite him to my ball."

"He was needed," Angelo replied. "And he will soon be needed again."

The Contessa shifted her gaze back to me. She took a few advancing steps, then came to a stop once more. I tried desperately to speak, to scream through the tight gag across my mouth, to make a last effort at convincing the Contessa that I was not Lucia. But the sounds that penetrated the thick gag were nothing more than gasps. I struggled once more with the bindings around my wrists, which were tied behind my back, but they would not give. I tried to get up but could not.

"I have done my part," Angelo said, so sharply it sent a chill through me. "Now it is up to you to finish it. The pistol shot won't be heard over the music and commotion downstairs. The guests will hear nothing."

The Contessa's eyes darted to Angelo, then she swung her head to look at me. Slowly, she continued to approach me. Her eyes never left my face. I tried once more to scream through the thick cloth over my mouth, but the scream died in my throat. My whole body became paralyzed with fear. I wanted to hurl myself away from where I was pressed against the wall, but my body would not respond.

The Contessa came to stand directly over me. She lowered her head. The hooded eyes peered into my face. She then stepped back two paces, studying me. A muscle twitched at the corner of the thin lips. She again darted a glance at Angelo, then slid her eyes to me.

The room had become very still. Cold perspiration trickled down my back. My pulse hammered.

"You did bring the pistol, didn't you?" Angelo said into the silence.

"Yes, I brought it," the Contessa answered as she drew the pistol out of her sleeve.

CHAPTER 13

"Then use it," Angelo said. "Why do you hesitate? I've done my part."

"Yes, Angelo. And you've done it well, haven't you?" the Contessa said with a side glance at him.

Returning her gaze to me, she stepped back two paces, her eyes on me, the pistol still held firmly between the long, bony fingers.

The room became intensely quiet.

My body jolted when, unexpectedly, Angelo's voice shattered the silence. "Will you do what has to be done?" he said in a firm, impatient tone. "I did what you asked me to do. I found her. There she is."

"Yes, Angelo, there she is," the Contessa said under her breath. "But she is not Lucia."

Angelo's eyes widened. He jerked from the reclining posture in the chair to an upright position and was about to speak, but the Contessa cut him off.

"No, Angelo, she is not Lucia. She is Miss Teresa Weston, an American from Boston." She raised her hand to silence Angelo when he attempted to protest. "I have seen her identification papers—baptismal certificate, First Communion diploma, even a letter of recommendation from a Boston museum where she was recently employed. A friend of Miss Teresa Weston's, one Charles Voulart, showed me the papers which she'd given him for safekeeping."

"It is a lie!" Angelo shouted. "You believe that lying Frenchman? He—"

Again, the Contessa silenced him with an abrupt gesture of

her hand. "No, Angelo, it is you who lied," she said in a low, calm voice. "You perpetrated a fraud. You knew that if you searched long enough you would find a look-alike. There was nothing distinctive about Lucia's appearance. My failing eyesight was also in your favor. How fortunate for you that Miss Teresa Weston spoke our Venetian language."

Angelo made another feeble attempt to protest, but at a fierce stare from the Contessa he fell back silent into his chair.

"And that story you told me," the Contessa went on, "about the five years in a Swiss sanatorium for a mental derangement. That was helpful, wasn't it? The amnesia also fitted nicely into your scheme."

"It's all true," Angelo cried. "Charles Voulart is the liar, not I. This is Lucia. She was in a Swiss sanatorium for five years. She did have amnesia. She still has. She had to be put away into that sanatorium because—"

"Yes, Lucia, indeed, was a patient in a Swiss sanatorium," the Contessa broke in. "She was a patient there because of a lung disease. I learned just this evening that Lucia died in that Swiss sanatorium."

"That isn't true," Angelo exclaimed, leaning forward, his hands gripping the arms of the chair.

"It *is* true, Angelo," the Contessa said. "But you continued to take money from me, pretending to be still searching for Lucia. As if I had not been giving you considerable amounts of money most of your life. But it was the large sum I'd promised you upon delivering Lucia to me that goaded you to this fraud. You couldn't bear to let that money slip away from you. You knew I was leaving you no inheritance. I've been made the victim of a fraud."

"It is not a fraud," Angelo said, his voice composed now. "It is Charles Voulart who is trying to defraud you."

The Contessa slowly shook her head. "It is you, Angelo, who tried to defraud me. It was Maria Cassiano who told me that Lucia is dead, that she died in that Swiss sanatorium."

"Maria Cassiano?" Angelo uttered in a hoarse whisper.

The Contessa nodded. "Yes, unknown to you, I invited her to my San Toto Ball. I'd intended to show off the Palazzo Rogatti to her, and especially, to show off Lucia to her. I wanted Maria Cassiano to learn tonight that I would have the last word about Lucia. I know that I have a fatal illness. I was not concerned about the consequences of my act. But it was Maria Cassiano who informed me of Lucia's death. And you know from past experience, don't you, Angelo, that Maria Cassiano could always ferret out any news. That was why you didn't want her to come to my ball. You were afraid she might have learned of Lucia's death.

"Even after Maria Cassiano told me that Lucia was dead, I could not bring myself to believe it was true. I'd waited such a long time to repay Lucia. But when Charles Voulart produced all those identification papers, I realized I'd been defrauded."

Angelo sprang out of his chair. "Let us go downstairs and face those two liars," he cried. "I dare Maria Cassiano and Charles Voulart to tell me she is not Lucia."

He began to go toward the door. The Contessa raised the hand which held the pistol and fired one shot. Angelo fell face down on the floor.

I could hear myself scream through the bindings over my mouth. My hands, tied behind my back, grasped the wall behind me in a desperate clawing motion. I tried to get up but could not.

The stepbrother uttered a choked gasp, then rushed to Angelo's side. He roughly turned him over and snatched a key from Angelo's shirt pocket.

The Contessa, who had been standing motionless, gazing at Angelo's still body, looked up as the stepbrother ran to the door. She raised her hand and fired the pistol while the stepbrother fumbled with the key. She misfired. The next instant the stepbrother was out the door. The Contessa raced after him. I heard their pounding footsteps along the marble corridor.

The stepbrother, in searching for the key, had turned Angelo's body to face me. The light brown eyes stared at me unseeing. The dark ringlets on his forehead appeared damp. His lips, slightly open, were turned up at the corners, mimicking the cherubic smile that so frequently had lighted up his face. Music from the grand salon floated down the corridor and filled the room.

After what seemed like hours but, no doubt, was only seconds, I heard voices and footsteps in the corridor. Then Charles strode into the room. He stopped short at the sight of Angelo's body. Then he was at my side, removing the tight band from around my mouth, freeing my hands and feet from the bindings.

"You're hurt," I said when he'd removed the gag from my mouth. His face was bruised and scratched. There was a wide, blood-dried gash on his chin.

"I'm all right," he answered as he lifted me gently into his arms. As he carried me out of the room I became aware of the swarm of people who had followed Charles into the room. The faces were all a blur, except for the Police Inspector, whom I had met before when he had called at the palazzo. He was leaning over Angelo's body, talking with another man in uniform.

Charles carried me to the adjoining room, which was my room, and placed me on the bed.

"Angelo is dead, isn't he?" I said.

"I believe he is."

"And the stepbrother?"

"As he raced along the corridor he ran directly into the arms of the Police Inspector."

"And the Contessa?"

"She collapsed. Looked like a heart seizure. Too much excitement for her."

Charles placed a pillow under my head. "Don't try to talk any more. The doctor will soon be here."

I gave myself over to the comfort of the bed. My hands and ankles stung and ached from the tight bindings. My lips were bruised from the gag. Charles produced a wet cloth from the bathroom and gently wiped my face.

I could hear the commotion in the adjoining room. Soon the Police Inspector's voice rose above the tumult. The guests, evidently, had become aware of what had occurred on the top floor and had streamed upstairs. Now they were being ordered back. The noise shifted to the corridor.

Gradually, the noise in the corridor subsided. The Police Inspector entered my room. "How is she?" he asked Charles.

"I'm all right," I answered. "I was frightened more than anything."

"There will be a doctor here soon," the Police Inspector said as he turned to leave.

"After which I hope she may be removed to the hotel where I am staying," Charles said to the Police Inspector. "A friend of my family, Signora Vittoria Scalzi, is also staying at the hotel. She will take care of Signorina Weston."

"That will be satisfactory," the Police Inspector said.

"Tell me what happened to you," I said to Charles when the Police Inspector left.

"Wouldn't you rather rest now and hear the details later?"

"Tell me now."

"I was about to get dressed for the ball," Charles began, pulling a chair to the bed, "when Angelo arrived. He said he had come to inquire about you, that you had not yet returned to the palazzo. Before I had a chance to reply, another man—his stepbrother, I learned later—barged into the room. He and Angelo silently but efficiently proceeded to nearly pound the life out of me. After they'd just about knocked me senseless, they tied me up. The last I saw of them before I became unconscious was Angelo and the stepbrother letting themselves out, carrying the ball costume."

"I thought it was you I saw in the pirate costume, hurrying across the grand salon," I said. "Shortly after that, a servant came to direct me to that fictitious gentleman from Mestre. A moment before the servant appeared, the Contessa had introduced me to Maria Cassiano—as Lucia. If I hadn't left immediately, Maria Cassiano would have told the Contessa then that I was not Lucia and—"

"No, I doubt that it would have worked out that easily," Charles said. "When I confronted the Contessa she'd already heard Maria Cassiano's explanation, but she refused to believe. It wasn't till I raced back to the hotel and brought with me your identification papers that the Contessa began to accept that you were not Lucia."

"After the Contessa saw my identification papers, then what?"

"Eventually, the Contessa seemed to be accepting the fact. She then said that Angelo had taken you to Fiora's house on the island of Murano. She said that Angelo wouldn't explain why. I didn't believe the Murano story and I intended to search the palazzo. But Matalda came to tell me that the Police Inspector had arrived. Before I returned to the hotel for your identification papers, I had told Matalda to summon the police and to have them wait in the kitchen so as not to arouse the guests. I decided then to have the Inspector accompany me when I went up to your room. When I joined him and another officer in the kitchen, I asked him to dispatch some officers to Fiora's house on the island of Murano. Matalda knew the address and she was sent to the police station with the message. The Police Inspector, after learning that you were missing, suggested we first search the cellars, the wine cellar in particular. He explained that when he'd visited the palazzo recently, the Contessa made some puzzling remarks about the wine cellar. Then he thought little of it, but now it would be wise to search there first. Of course, we only wasted precious time.

"When the Police Inspector, his assistant, and I emerged

from the cellars, we were just in time to see the Contessa going toward the back stairway. The Police Inspector stopped her. The Contessa did not appear perturbed. She explained that, thinking back to something Angelo had said, he might be holding you captive in your room, although she couldn't imagine why. She said she was going up to talk to Angelo.

"I was poised to rush up the stairs ahead of the Contessa, but the Police Inspector and his assistant held me back. I was told that I would only provoke Angelo, possibly precipitate violence. He said he had complete confidence in the Contessa. I remembered what you'd said about him when he'd visited the palazzo, how bedazzled he was by the Contessa. He obviously thought her incapable of any wrongdoing. But then, I didn't consider the Contessa the dangerous one. It was Angelo who concerned me. Maria Cassiano held the same view. She said if there was any mischief, it would be Angelo's doing. She was puzzled by your presence at the ball but saw nothing sinister in it.

"I wondered, too, about that gentleman from Mestre. I thought he might be held captive along with you, that Angelo was trying to get information from him. At that stage, I didn't think your resemblance to Lucia was the crucial thing but that everything—as you had claimed—was connected with information concerning Dominic, information that Angelo urgently wanted.

"And so the Contessa went upstairs alone," I said.

"Yes, the Police Inspector was confident that she would be able to deal with Angelo. After she had been gone a long time, the Police Inspector started up the stairs, instructing me and his assistant to do so quietly. He then ordered us to wait at the top of the stairs while he crept along the corridor and listened at various doors. He returned to report that the Contessa and Angelo were having a conversation in one of the rooms on the top floor.

"It was what sounded like two pistol shots that brought us running. Halfway along the corridor, the stepbrother raced right into the arms of the Police Inspector. The Contessa lunged out of the room. She raised her hand to fire the pistol but she slumped against the wall, clawed at it, then collapsed. I rushed into the room, leaving the Contessa to the Police Inspector's assistant."

Charles stopped and looked at me questioningly. "Now perhaps you can enlighten me. I'm still not clear why the Contessa shot Angelo or what all this about Lucia means."

Briefly, I explained what Angelo had related to me shortly before the Contessa arrived with the pistol.

"She wanted the privilege of killing Lucia after Angelo lured her to the palazzo?" Charles said. "And Angelo was to be paid handsomely for this?"

"That was the plan. And the Contessa further wished to flaunt this before Maria Cassiano. The Contessa didn't care that she would be accused of murder. She knew she had a fatal illness. When Angelo learned that the real Lucia had died, he decided he was not going to be deprived of what he called the prize money, so he searched for a look-alike. The original plan was that I was to be killed—by the Contessa— the day I arrived at the palazzo. Angelo got into difficulty when the Contessa decided she wished to enact her vengeance during a San Toto Ball."

"Now what about you?" I said. "How did you manage to get to the palazzo after Angelo and his stepbrother had beaten you and tied you up?"

"After I regained consciousness, I kept on struggling with the bindings on my hands. I couldn't call for help. They'd placed a gag over my mouth. Gradually, by persistence, I managed to free myself. I couldn't enlist Signora Scalzi's help. She'd gone to Torcello and wouldn't return to Venice until the next morning.

"Thinking back, I'm sorry I didn't listen to you when you first expressed worry about remaining at the palazzo," Charles said, "and I'm sorry I listened to the Police Inspector and didn't rush up those stairs ahead of the Contessa."

"You wouldn't have got into the room anyway. The door was locked and Angelo had the key. Perhaps Angelo had a pistol too. No, I think the Police Inspector was right. You might have provoked Angelo into panic. Things might have turned out even worse. Remember, the Contessa was carrying a concealed pistol. If you'd become a real threat to her, she might have shot you."

Charles and I looked toward the doorway. The Police Inspector entered with the doctor. Charles and the Inspector then excused themselves.

After the doctor had attended to me, I inquired whether Angelo was dead. The doctor said he was. "And the stepbrother?" I asked. "Wounded in the shoulder," the doctor replied. "He is now in the hands of the police." "And the Contessa?" I asked. "A heart seizure," the doctor answered. "She is in a bad way."

As the doctor was leaving, I requested that he take care of Charles, who appeared to be in greater need of medical attention than I.

By the time Charles returned to sit beside my bed, I was so drowsy from the sleeping draught the doctor had given me, that I could not keep my eyes open.

When, later, I awoke, I found Signora Vittoria Scalzi sitting beside my bed. The room was flooded with sunlight. "It is morning," she said, smiling, patting my arm lightly. "Charles will return soon. He sent for me early this morning," she explained. "I am still staying at the hotel here in Venice. When Charles returns—he's with the Inspector now —he and I will take you to the hotel where you will stay a while with me."

Matalda entered bearing coffee and croissants. Her face was pale, her eyes red-rimmed. Orsola, she said, was inconsolable about Angelo's death. "And the Contessa," she murmured with a lift of her shoulders, "she is half dead, lying in her bed like a gray corpse."

She came to stand beside my bed and regarded me intently.

"Signorina, you do not believe the terrible thing the Contessa is accused of, do you? You know the Contessa could never do such a terrible thing. It is all lies." She paused, her eyes filling with tears. "Now she lies in her bed like one already dead. But I will take care of her." She turned away slowly and left the room, her steps slow and heavy.

Shortly afterward, Charles arrived to take me away from the palazzo. All of Dominic's belongings and my few possessions were taken with me. Signora Scalzi helped me to dress—in the travel clothes in which I'd arrived in Venice.

As the gondola slid away from the striped mooring pole, I looked back at the Palazzo Rogatti. Swirls of dull gray fog clung to the walls of the palazzo, almost obliterating it from view.

For the following three days I was a guest of Vittoria Scalzi in her hotel suite. The first two days she insisted that I spend much of my time in bed or just lazing about. The third day I was sufficiently recovered to go to Vicenza with Charles to say good-bye to Uncle Niccolo.

Upon arrival in Vicenza, we learned that Uncle Niccolo had returned to Padua to work for his previous employer, and we were given the address.

"I've given up the thought of owning my own horse-breeding farm," Uncle Niccolo said. "I'm too old to get myself involved in such an enterprise. I'm truly content now that my old employer has taken me back. I am doing the work I enjoy and do not have to worry about all the responsibility."

Uncle Niccolo took Charles and me to visit with various relatives in Padua. It was during a conversation with one of the relatives that I learned the identity of the "prominent Venetian family" which Dominic had mentioned in his letter to me. Dominic had visited the relative after his quarrel with Uncle Niccolo. It was he who had suggested that Dominic get in touch with a man who owned a shop in Venice and dealt with various art objects.

"I'd become acquainted with the man when I lived in Venice," the relative explained. "I thought he might be helpful to Dominic, although I wasn't quite sure what Dominic had in mind."

Upon our return to Venice, Charles and I went to the shop, which turned out to be one of the shops in the Merceria, where, the day of the San Toto Ball, we had spent some time browsing among the art objects. The shop owner confirmed the story. He was acquainted with the man in Padua and, yes, Dominic had come to him for assistance. "He seemed like a young man with talent," the shop owner told us, "and I promised to help him. Unfortunately, I soon learned that the young man, although a fine portrait painter, had no business sense and he had some rather immature ideas about how one went about making one's fortune. I came to the decision, eventually, that I would have to tell him that I could not help him, but—then I learned of his death. I was deeply grieved by that. I am sorry, signorina. He was a likable young man."

We thanked the man, and as I left the shop I felt a sense of relief. I would no longer have to wonder who the "prominent Venetian family" was and I was now certain that Dominic had not fallen prey to some questionable business dealings. As Uncle Niccolo had said, Dominic simply had no head for business.

From the shop, Charles took me to San Michele. I remained at Dominic's grave for some time, knowing I might never see it again.

From there we went to the Piazza San Marco. Sitting in front of Florian's, drinking coffee, I said to Charles, "This, more or less, is how it all began. It doesn't seem possible that it was only two weeks ago. Now I must return home to America."

"There is nothing and no one for you to go home to," Charles said.

"I cannot stay in Venice."

"No, not in Venice. To come here occasionally, yes, but not to live here."

"Then where?"

Charles placed his hand over mine on the table. "Let me begin, Teresa, by answering a question you put to me several days ago. I arrived at the Palazzo Rogatti one day in a particularly happy mood—"

"I remember," I said. "I asked you whether you'd had some good news. I said you looked as if you'd had some burden or obstacle removed."

Charles nodded, smiling. "There is a certain young lady," he explained. "Her father is a business associate of my father's. It had been decided from the time we were quite young that eventually she and I would marry. All along I'd felt we weren't right for each other. Yet, when you arrived in Venice, the wedding preparations were in full swing.

"Forgive me for bringing this up now, Teresa, so soon after your fiancé's death, but it must be said. I fell in love with you. I confronted my parents and announced to their shocked surprise that the wedding must be called off. There was considerable consternation, of course, in both my family and hers. Then, as a further surprise, we all learned that the young lady was not eager for the marriage. Like me, she'd drifted into it.

"I won't talk to you about love and marriage now, Teresa," Charles said, "not under the circumstances. But give us time. Don't go away. Vittoria Scalzi is returning today to her villa near Rome. She would like to have you as her guest. Then I want you to come to Switzerland to meet my parents. I've already told them about you and they wish to meet you. You'll like them. I know they'll like you."

I looked at him, bewildered, not knowing how to answer. I'd become aware of a growing feeling for him but, as he himself had said, "under the circumstances" I never let the feeling take hold. *Give us time.* Yes, with time, my feelings for Charles would no longer need to be kept hidden.

Charles gazed at me, waiting for my answer.

I 25

I placed my hand over his. "I'll stay, Charles. I'll come to Switzerland with you."

He smiled, then he took my hands firmly in his. We would face the future together. We sat like that for a long while, hands tightly clasped. No words were needed.

Stories by Helen York have appeared in the New York *Daily News* and *Family Star*. Ms. York was formerly a French teacher and also worked in a law office before devoting full time to her writing. She is the author of *Tremorra Towers*, also published by Doubleday.